CATHERINE GEORGE
Tangled Emotions

Harlequin®

TORONTO NEW YORK LONDON
AMSTERDAM PARIS SYDNEY HAMBURG
STOCKHOLM ATHENS TOKYO MILAN MADRID
PRAGUE WARSAW BUDAPEST AUCKLAND

Recycling programs
for this product may
not exist in your area.

ISBN-13: 978-0-373-74149-6

TANGLED EMOTIONS

First North American Publication 2011

www.Harlequin.com

Printed in U.S.A.

Catherine George was born in Wales, and early on developed a passion for reading, which eventually fuelled her compulsion to write. Marriage to an engineer led to nine years in Brazil, but on his later travels the education of her son and daughter kept her in the U.K. Instead of constant reading to pass her lonely evenings, she began to write the first of her romantic novels. When not writing and reading she loves to cook, listen to opera and browse in antiques shops.

CHAPTER ONE

SOMEONE was following her. The narrow street was deserted, and the light at the end still broken, which meant a plunge into total darkness before she was safe behind a locked door. Determined not to look round, she lengthened her stride, wishing she'd waited for a taxi. The starless night was hot and humid, but for the first time in her life she felt a cold stab of fear. She dismissed it scornfully: once she reached the house, whoever was following would just walk past. Then found herself proved horribly wrong when two skinny figures in cartoon masks appeared on either side of her, jostling her to a standstill.

'Give us money and you won't get hurt,' squeaked one of them, grabbing her arm.

'Not a chance!' she hissed, and, fired by fear and rage and sheer incredulity that this could actually be happening to her, she rammed an elbow into her young assailant's ribs and prepared to do battle.

* * *

After a two-hour drive on the motorway, diversion signs were leading Joe Tregenna all round
the town, and he was in no mood to get involved
when his headlamps picked up a knot of youths in
a brawl. Then he saw that one of them was a girl,
struggling with two figures in masks. With a muttered curse he braked to a stop and jumped from
the car just as one youth doubled up in a crumpled
heap on the ground and the other took to his heels
and raced off, sobbing, in the darkness.

'Are you all right?' Joe asked the girl urgently.
'Are you hurt?'

She shook her head, thrusting her hair behind
her ears. 'No,' she panted. 'Just livid. But *he's* not
so good.' She glared at the gasping, writhing figure
on the ground. 'I'd better ring the police.'

At the dreaded word the boy shot to his feet, but
Joe grabbed him by his collar. 'Oh, no, you don't,
sunshine.'

'We wasn't hurting her,' the boy choked. 'We
was only asking for change.'

'In masks?' said Joe grimly. 'I don't think so.'
He turned to the girl. 'You're shivering. Are you
sure you're all right?'

She nodded brusquely. 'Angry, not cold.'

Joe reached one-handed for the cellphone on his
belt. 'Ring the police on this.'

'*No!*' The boy burst into tears, shaking like a
leaf in Joe's grasp. 'Please don't turn me in, miss.

We got the masks at the garage with some sweets, so when we saw you come out of the pub we followed you for a dare—got the idea from the telly,' he sobbed. 'My mum'll *kill* me.'

She surveyed him in silence for a moment, arms folded. 'Let him go,' she said at last.

Joe stared at her incredulously. 'You can't let him get away with it!'

She moved towards the boy, who shrank away in fright. 'You just listen to me,' she said militantly. 'Here's the deal. I'll leave the police out of it if you swear you won't do this again. Ever.'

He nodded feverishly. 'I won't. Nor Dean won't, neither.'

'Is Dean your friend?' she asked.

He shook his head, sniffing hard. 'Kid brother. He didn't want to come. He was scared.'

'What's your name?'

'Robbie.'

'Right, then, Robbie,' she said brusquely. 'No more stupid stunts like this.' She bent to pick up the fallen mask. 'But I'll keep Batman here. It'll have your DNA on it, remember. Is your mother at home?'

He shook his head. 'She's a nurse at the General—on nights this week.'

'She leaves you on your own at night?' said Joe, frowning.

'*No*, never!' The boy knuckled tears from his

eyes. 'Our stepdad's home in bed. We climbed out the bedroom window once he was snoring.'

'Are you in the habit of this?'

He gulped. 'No, honest. We never done it before.'

'And you'd better be sure you never do it again, like the lady said,' ordered Joe. 'I'm sure you've been warned about lifts from strangers, so we'll walk you home and hand you over to your step-father,' he added, sending the boy into hysterics again.

'Are you afraid of him?' said the girl sharply.

'No! He's a good bloke. But he'll grass on me to *Mum*!'

When the boy pleaded to climb back through his bedroom window instead of waking his step-father, Joe raised an eyebrow at the tall, watchful figure of the girl. 'OK with you? I'll walk you home afterwards.'

The girl nodded. 'Fine. Come on, then, Robbie. Let's go.'

When they arrived at the address Robbie gave them, the boy gave a sigh of relief when he saw a face peering round a curtain at an upstairs window.

'Dean's back! He run straight home like I said.'

'Sensible chap,' said Joe, and turned a stern look on the boy. 'Now, just you remember, my lad,' he said with deliberate menace. 'I know where you live.'

Robbie nodded feverishly, then ran up the path, swarmed up a drainpipe as nimbly as a monkey, and disappeared head-first through the open window.

Joe waited until he was sure the boy was safe inside, then gave a wry glance at his companion as they began the walk back. 'Hello, at last. My name's Joe Tregenna.'

She smiled briefly. 'Fen Dysart. Thanks for your help.'

'When I spotted a fight I was going to drive on by, or call the police at the very most,' he said frankly. 'But when I saw two lads to one girl I thought I'd better wade in. But I was superfluous. You'd sorted them before I could even get out of the car.'

'No big deal with a pair of kids. I'm a head taller than either of them, for a start.' She shrugged. 'It was just reflex. I lashed out at them in sheer temper.'

'Which could have been dangerous with a couple of real criminals,' he pointed out. 'Lucky for you it *was* a pair of kids behind those masks.'

'Which is why I laid into them,' she said curtly, then frowned. 'How old do you think Robbie is?'

'Hard to say. Old enough to know better,

certainly. Where do you live? Can I drive you there?'

'No need. I'm just down the road from my adventure, in Farthing Street. Once we reach your car I'll be fine,' she added. 'No need for you to come any further.'

But Joe insisted on seeing her right to the door of her small, end-of-terrace house. 'Will there be anyone there?'

'No.'

'In that case I'll see you safely inside before I go on my way.'

About to refuse, Fen changed her mind. A little company right this minute wasn't a bad idea. Now that the episode was over she felt a bit shaky. She went round the house to the back, unlocked a door, and switched on the light in a small, bare kitchen. Then she turned to get a look at her companion, who returned the scrutiny with equal curiosity as he closed the door behind him.

Joe Tregenna was a few inches taller than her own five feet ten, slim-hipped and broad-shouldered. He wore his dishevelled brown hair long enough to curl slightly at the ends, and his eyes were a dark enough blue to look black at first glance. Like his mouth, they held a hint of humour rather at odds with the uncompromising cut of nose and chin. He wore a formal white shirt with a tie loosened at the open collar, and linen trousers that looked like part of a suit.

'I need coffee,' she said abruptly, aware she was staring, and thrust back hair even more dishevelled than his. 'How about you?'

'Please.' He smiled. 'I could do with some caffeine after the encounter with Pennington's junior underworld.'

'Take a seat. I won't be long.' Fen dumped her backpack, shrugged off her denim jacket and slung it on the back of a chair, then filled the kettle and plugged it in. She took mugs from a cupboard and milk from the refrigerator, aware all the time that Joe Tregenna's eyes were following her every move. Not that she minded. After charging to her rescue like Sir Galahad he was entitled to a good look at the maiden in distress.

She made coffee, set the mugs on the table, and sat down opposite her visitor, who chuckled suddenly.

'What's the joke?' she asked.

'I know where you live! I can't believe I actually said that to the little tyke.' He grinned at her. 'Though you weren't far behind, with your talk of deals and DNA.'

'The idea was to frighten him in terms from his beloved "telly". He obviously likes cop shows. So between us let's hope we've diverted our Robbie

from a life of crime.' Fen shrugged. 'No way could
I have handed him over to the police.'

He looked at her thoughtfully as he drank some
coffee. 'Do you make a habit of walking home
alone late at night?'

'Asking for trouble, you mean?' she retorted.
'No, I don't. My car's in for repairs. And like a fool
I didn't think to ring for a taxi until I'd finished
work. By then my customers had snaffled them
all, which meant a forty-minute wait.'

'Customers?'

'I work behind the bar at the Mitre.'

He shook his head. 'I'm fairly new in town. I
don't know that one.'

'It's a big place on the crossroads, near the area
where we dropped Robbie. It used to be a coach-
ing inn, now it's the "in" place of the moment and
very busy.' Fen shrugged. 'Which is how I got the
job. They were desperate for staff.'

'How long have you worked there?'

She smiled ruefully. 'Long enough to know that
a trudge home is bad news after a double shift on
my feet. In future I drive or take taxis.'

'I'm glad to hear it.' He finished his coffee and
got up. 'It's a bad idea for any woman to walk
alone at night. And for someone with your looks
it's madness,' he added casually.

Fen took her looks for granted. But Joe
Tregenna's offhand remark pleased her rather a

lot. Even with the sting in the tail. 'It's not a habit of mine, Mr Tregenna.'

He raised an eyebrow. 'Can't we cut the formality?'

'Right. Thank you, Joe.' She smiled, and held out her hand.

He held on to it for a second. 'I was only too glad to help—' He broke off as the phone at his belt began beeping. 'Excuse me.'

Fen busied herself with rinsing the coffee mugs, doing her best to block her ears to what was obviously not the happiest of conversations.

'For the last time, Melissa,' she heard Joe say eventually. 'I was delayed. I'm not even home yet. I'll ring you tomorrow. Goodnight.' He looked at Fen. 'Sorry about that,' he said brusquely, putting the phone back. 'I forgot to ring the lady I dined with.'

'Tell her it was my fault.'

He shook his head, the humour back in his eyes. 'Somehow, Miss Fen Dysart, I think that would do far more harm than good.'

'If that's a compliment, thank you.' She hesitated for a moment, then gave in to curiosity and asked what had brought him to Pennington.

'I sell insurance.'

'Really?' she said, surprised it wasn't something more high-powered. 'Thanks again for coming to my rescue.'

'My pleasure.' He paused. 'Do you live here alone?'

'Yes.'

'Then make sure you lock up securely behind me. Goodnight.'

Because her new home had no shower, Fen was rinsing her hair clean under the bathroom taps when reaction finally caught up with her. Shivering, she pulled the plug, hopped out of the coffin-like tub and wrapped herself in a towelling robe. She switched her hairdryer to the hottest setting, and the moment her hair was dry enough pulled on pyjamas for once and burrowed under the covers. But she took a long time to get to sleep. And when she did dreams woke her and rocketed her bolt upright, sweating and scrabbling for the light switch as she heaped curses on young Robbie's head for giving her nightmares.

'You look a bit fragile, Fen,' said the owner of the Mitre next morning.

She explained about the near-mugging of the night before, and got bawled out by Tim Mathias for not asking someone for a lift home.

'I didn't think about it until it was too late. Anyway, I get the car back this afternoon, so no more transport problems.'

Once the lunchtime session was over Fen went to collect her car, then drove back to the Mitre to find Tim using the full battery of his charm on some of his female staff. When Fen asked what was going there was a ripple of laughter and one of them pointed a dramatic finger at her.

'Fen's your best bet, Tim,' said Jilly, grinning. 'She can do it, no problem.'

'Do what?' demanded Fen with suspicion.

Tim eyed his newest recruit speculatively. 'You know that this is live music night in the piano bar?'

She nodded. 'But if Martin's off sick it's no use asking me to fill in; I can't play a note.'

'Martin's fine. The problem is Diane, our sexy songstress.' Tim scowled. 'She's lost her voice. We'll have her fans streaming in to spend good money on drinks, but when they find her missing they probably won't stay to buy more. How the devil did the woman manage to lose her voice in the middle of a heat wave?'

'I don't suppose she did it on purpose—' Fen broke off, staring at him as the penny dropped. 'Wait a minute. Why are you looking at me?'

'I've heard you singing when no one's around— not bad at all, in a breathless kind of way.' Tim grinned. 'Come on, Fen. It's only tonight. I'll get Martin to come in for a quick run-through, now while it's quiet, then tonight you just croon a few standards into a microphone for a couple of sets. Easy as pie.'

Laughing at the loud encouragement from her joshing colleagues, she shook her head. 'Not a chance. I'm not good enough.'

'Of course you are. We're not talking grand opera. And,' he added coaxingly, 'I'll pay you double your money.'

Fen's eyebrows rose. 'You mean that?'

Tim laid a hand on his heart. 'Would I lie?'

She thought it over, reminding herself why she'd come here asking for a job at the Mitre in the first place. This would add fuel to the fire. And she could certainly do with the money. 'All right, I'll do it. But for one night only,' she added, to cheers from the others.

'Done,' said Tim jubilantly. 'Remember Michelle Pfeiffer in *The Fabulous Baker Boys*?'

'Certainly not. I'm too young!' Fen grinned. 'Actually, I do remember. But I'm a lanky brunette, not a fragile blonde, and I don't have a shiny red dress.' She glanced down at her uniform white blouse and black skirt. 'Talking of dresses, I suppose I won't do as I am?'

'Hell, no,' said Tim bluntly. 'Surely you can come up with something sexy, like the stuff Diane wears?'

'A beanpole like me?' she jeered. 'I don't do sexy. But if I can dash home after my session with Martin, I'll find something.'

'Take a couple of hours. You're not due on until eight-thirty.'

The rehearsal went well enough to earn Fen a round of applause from everyone in earshot as the staff prepared for the evening. She got by largely because the songs were familiar, her memory for lyrics was good, and Martin was a skilful, sympathetic accompanist who gave useful tips on how to steal a breath in certain places. But, with her ears buzzing with Gershwin standards on the way to the car park later, doubts set in.

She had to be mad! The adventures of the night before had obviously addled her brain. Martin had assured her that her husky, breathless style was very easy on the ear, but it was sheer audacity, just the same, to perform for an audience used to an experienced performer like Diane. On the other hand, Fen thought philosophically, she could never resist a challenge.

Back at the house, she scribbled the lyrics on a sheet of paper small enough to hide on top of the piano, in case she dried, then took a critical look at a brief, clinging black dress with narrow straps holding up the low cowled top. Deciding it would have to do, Fen took a breather with a sandwich and a mug of coffee before her bath, then began transforming herself into a cabaret act.

She applied an extra layer of foundation and blusher, accentuated her eyes with smoky green shadow and two coats of mascara, then brushed her curling dark hair loose on her shoulders. She surveyed the result in the mirror. The dress clung to her boyishly narrow hips, added a touch of welcome emphasis to her breasts, and left a lot of suntanned leg bare. Fen shrugged. Not bad, though a lot different from voluptuous blonde Diane, who was given to plunging necklines and glittery dresses long enough to hide her thick ankles.

When Fen arrived back at the Mitre, Jilly followed her into the staffroom and let out a loud whistle of appreciation.

'Gosh, Fen, you look terrific. I never noticed your eyes were green before. Diane would be mad as fire if she could see you.'

'I'm more concerned with how I'll sound than the way I look!' said Fen, exchanging trainers for stilt-heeled black sandals.

'Don't worry.' Jilly patted her on the shoulder. 'The male punters will be too busy looking at those gorgeous tanned legs to care, dearie.'

Tim Mathias was equally enthusiastic when Fen reported for duty. 'You look fantastic,' he said jubilantly. 'Thanks a lot. There's a bigger crowd than usual in there tonight.'

'You'll be fine,' Martin assured her, when Fen handed him her crib sheet of lyrics.

'Can you hide them where I can take a look if I forget?' she said urgently.

'Will do.' He patted her shoulder, glanced at his watch, and made for the door. 'I'm on. See you in a few minutes.'

'Want a drink, Fen?' said Tim.

'No, thanks.' Fen took in a deep, unsteady breath as the sound of Martin's piano came through the speakers. 'I just hope I don't make a hash of it.'

'You'll be fine.' Tim smiled encouragingly as a skilled arpeggio from Martin finished his short selection from the shows. 'There's your cue. Break a leg.'

Fen waited, heart hammering, at the back of the small piano stage, while Martin apologised for Diane's indisposition, then gave the audience the glad news that at the last minute another *artiste* had been persuaded to sing for them instead.

'Let's have a big hand for the lovely Fenella!'

Fen experienced a surge of unadulterated panic, survived it, heaved in a deep breath and stepped, smiling, onto the small, raised platform.

Martin gave her an encouraging wink as he began the familiar opening to a Gershwin melody. Fen smiled at him gratefully, checked that her crib sheet was in place, leaned into the curve of the grand piano, and began to sing.

At the end of the third song the applause was loud and enthusiastic, with shouts of 'Encore'.

Martin promised more later instead, and took Fen's hand to bow.

Back in the office Fen sat down abruptly, her knees trembling now the first hurdle was over.

'That was just brilliant, Fen,' said Tim, elated. 'You went over really well. Drink?'

'Just water, please—I got rather hot in there.'

Martin grinned. 'You weren't the only one. When you pleaded for someone to watch over you quite a few blokes in there were panting to volunteer. One, in particular, couldn't take his eyes off you.'

'I was too busy concentrating to notice,' said Fen, and drained the glass thirstily.

Tim looked worried as he told Martin about the mugging incident the night before. 'You be extra careful tonight, Fen.'

'One thing you can be sure of, boss dear. I'm in no danger from my mugger of last night,' she assured him. 'He's probably tucked up in bed by now.'

When Martin left them to do his second stint at the piano Grace Mathias came in to add her congratulations.

'You were a big hit, Fen. Quite a few of my diners went off to the piano bar afterwards.' She smiled at her husband. 'While they paid their bills I casually mentioned that we had a new attraction tonight.'

'What a businesswoman you are,' he said fondly.

'So get me a glass of something extravagant while I listen in peace to Fen's second set,' she said promptly.

'Don't expect too much, Grace,' warned Fen as she renewed her lipstick. 'Peggy Lee I'm not.' She jumped to her feet, tugged the clinging dress into place, then braced herself as her cue came through the sound system. 'That's me. Wish me luck.'

This time round Fen felt less nervous when she joined Martin at the piano. She smiled into the audience, which had grown considerably since the first set, then caught sight of a familiar face at the entrance, and instead of leaning against the grand piano perched herself on top of it as Martin began the introduction to a classic Cole Porter favourite. They followed it with Jerome Kern, then ended the set with Hoagy Carmichael's 'Skylark', which taxed Fen's untrained voice to the limit as she breathed, rather than sang, the last three ascending notes. Afterwards the applause was wildly enthusiastic, with loud demands for encores. But Fen shook her head, smiling, and kissed her hand to them as Martin, grinning from ear to ear, helped her down.

She felt drained as he took her back to receive warm thanks from Tim and Grace, plus some teasing from the three of them about her perch on the piano for the second set.

'I thought I'd give the punters value for money,' Fen said airily. She refused offers of drinks, accepted her fee, confirmed that her car was parked right outside the door, said her goodnights, then went off to exchange a word with some of the other girls before leaving.

When she reached the side door later Fen's heart gave a thump. A tall man stood barring her way, as expected. She stared up defiantly into dark eyes which held such furious disapproval she felt a surge of triumph. 'Hi,' she said casually. 'I didn't know you were coming here tonight.'

'Obviously,' he said through his teeth. 'What the *hell* do you think you're playing at?'

'Not playing. Working for my living.' Fen brushed past him, heading for the door, but he caught her by the hand and swung her round.

'Not so fast, my girl—'

'Problems, Fen?' said a familiar voice, and she turned to find Joe Tregenna smiling at her. 'Is this guy giving you trouble?'

'It's OK, Joe. No problem,' said Fen, freeing herself. 'He's a relative.'

Adam Dysart controlled himself with obvious effort. 'Look,' he said to Joe Tregenna, 'this is a family thing. Would you excuse us? I need to talk to Fenny.'

'But I don't want to talk to you,' she retorted, and smiled warmly at Joe as she took his hand. 'Thanks for coming to take me home.'

'My pleasure,' he said, without missing a beat. 'Won't you introduce us?'

'Unnecessary,' said Fen curtly, and, turning her back on Adam Dysart, she hurried Joe off.

'Sorry to land you in it again, Joe,' she muttered, casting a look behind her. 'A bit late in the day to ask, I know, but are you on your own?'

'Fortunately, yes,' he said, amused.

'That's a relief.' She smiled at him. 'This is a bit cheeky of me, but could you possibly drive me round for a bit? I don't want Adam to know where I live.'

'Of course. Better still, why not come to my place for a drink until the coast is clear?' said Joe as he led her to his car. 'Unless—'

'Unless what?' she asked absently, straining to see if Adam was in sight.

'Unless that guy's your husband. Because if so I'm not getting involved.'

She glared at him. 'Adam Dysart is most definitely not my husband. He's—' She halted, suddenly deflated. 'He's just a cousin.'

CHAPTER TWO

'AND not a kissing cousin, obviously,' observed Joe as he drove off. 'I stuck my oar in again in case he got rough with you.'

'No danger of that,' Fen assured him. 'I'm not in Adam's good books at the moment. But he would never harm me.'

'Why was he so angry with you?'

She sighed. 'I can't tell you that. Which is pretty mean, I know, when you've come to my rescue two nights running. Not,' she added militantly, 'that I couldn't have handled it myself—both times.'

'It didn't look that way to me.'

'You're wrong. I really can take care of myself.' She glanced at him curiously. 'I was so furious with Adam I forgot to ask why you were at the Mitre tonight, Joe. Were you eating there?'

'No. I called in on the chance that a certain bar person might serve me a drink, and to my surprise found she was doing a cabaret act.' Joe grinned. 'You didn't mention that last night.'

'I didn't know last night!' she said with feeling. 'The manager sprung it on me today because the usual *chanteuse* was careless enough to lose her voice. The piano bar does a roaring trade on the nights Diane sings, so rather than lose good business Tim bribed me to fill in.'

'How?'

'By paying double my usual wages. Which I don't deserve, because I can't sing as well as Diane.'

'From where I was standing your punters didn't agree. You went down very well indeed.'

'Flattery, Mr Tregenna?'

'Fact. The husky, breathless voice charmed them right enough, but it was the bare shoulders and endless legs that knocked 'em dead.'

Instead of taking offence Fen threw back her head and laughed. 'I just can't believe I did it. Any of it. I must have been out of my mind.'

'But tonight a star was born!'

'Not on your life.' She shook her head emphatically. 'I'm never doing that again. My nerves wouldn't stand it. Besides, when the lovely Diane hears what happened I bet her voice will make a dramatic recovery.'

Joe slanted a look at her. 'Pity. I enjoyed the show.'

Fen's eyebrows rose when he parked outside one of the most exclusive addresses in Pennington, most unlike her own narrow little back street. Joe Tregenna lived in a square with well-kept gardens, in an expensive part of town where roads were tree-lined, all the lights worked, and most of the large houses had been converted into luxury flats.

'This is it,' he said, helping her out of the car.

Fen looked up, impressed, at the creamy façade of a villa with arched triple windows and lace-like ironwork railings and balcony.

'It's not all mine,' said Joe. 'I live upstairs. But my neighbours on the ground floor are away a lot, so I get the garden to myself when time and weather permit.'

He unlocked a side door and led the way up a narrow flight of stairs to usher Fen into a big room with floor-to-ceiling windows and curtains drawn back on the walls, so that only the wrought-iron balcony outside hampered a view of the lamplit gardens in the square. In front of the Adam-style fireplace two sofas covered in chestnut cord faced each other in splendid isolation on the expanse of pale carpet.

'What a great room!' said Fen, impressed. 'I've never been in one of these houses before.' She grinned at him. 'You must have felt a bit claustro-phobic in my place last night.'

'Have you lived there long?'

'No. I intended sharing a flat originally, but changed my mind. So I rent my little terraced house instead.' She eyed him curiously. 'But if you live here, what brought you down my street last night?'

'Multiple roadworks. I'm new to Pennington, and somewhere among the diversion signs I took a wrong turning.' His eyes met hers. 'I'm glad I did. Otherwise it might have been a different story for you.'

'Not at all,' she said tartly. 'I had it all in hand before you even got out of your car.'

Joe looked unconvinced. 'Just the same, you might consider giving up night wanderings, Miss Dysart.'

'I already have,' she agreed soberly. 'I've learned my lesson, believe me.'

'Good. So what would you like to drink?' His eyes gleamed. 'Do *artistes* like you demand pink champagne?'

Fen let out a gurgle of laughter. 'No way would I describe myself as an *artiste*. And I'd prefer tea to pink champagne.'

'Then come with me.' Joe took her along the hall to a galley-style kitchen, which by daylight, he informed her, enjoyed a view of the back garden through the full-length window.

Fen sat down at the rectangle of marble which served as a kitchen table, and watched her host make tea in a chunky white pot. He shot her a look as he took mugs from a cupboard.

'Why the wry little smile?'

'It just occurred to me that I had the most colossal cheek in latching on to you tonight.'

He chuckled. 'I was glad to oblige. You've given me a couple of very entertaining evenings, Miss Dysart.'

'Not all down to me. You had dinner in London before you ran into me last night,' Fen reminded him. 'Did you live there before you came here?'

He nodded. 'But when the firm opened a branch in Pennington, I volunteered to relocate.'

'Because you fancied a change?'

'That too. But I'm single, with no children to uproot, so I was an obvious choice to make a move.'

Single, but not unattached, thought Fen with a touch of regret. 'Shall I pour tea for you, or are you having something stronger?'

'Tea. I'll wait until I get back for a nightcap.'

'By the way, did you manage to make peace with your lady?'

'No.' Joe's eyes shuttered. 'I had an illuminating—and unpleasant—little exchange with Melissa earlier on, which is why I went to the Mitre for a drink afterwards.'

'That bad?' said Fen with sympathy.

'Not good.' He looked at her for a moment. 'Would it bore you to hear the details?'

'Not in the least,' she said truthfully. 'Did she break up with you?'

'No, quite the reverse. Melissa took me by surprise. She'd been trying to persuade me to keep on my London flat for weekends all along, but last night I learned why. She took it for granted she could just move from her flat into mine.' His face hardened. 'She informed me it was pointless to go on paying good money for rent on her flat when my place would be empty during the week.'

Nice lady, thought Fen. 'You didn't want that?'

'No. Something she refused to believe over dinner last night. So to avoid a scene in the restaurant I put her in a taxi and drove straight here.' He shrugged. 'But tonight I explained, in words of one syllable, that the sale of the London flat was needed to finance this place, at which point she flew off the handle and told me she had no intention of burying herself in the back of beyond, even for me.'

'Ah,' said Fen, privately thinking that anyone who looked on Pennington as the back of beyond was best given up as a bad job. 'Has she seen this flat?'

Joe shook his head and refilled her mug. 'No.'

She smiled up at him. 'It might change her mind if she did.'

'No point. I've never thought of her as my "lady",

as you put it, so I made it very clear,' he said, his voice extra-dry, 'that her sacrifice was not, and never had been, required.'

'Ouch!'

'Exactly. Melissa went through the roof, exposing a side to her personality kept firmly under wraps before. Which is why I felt in urgent need of a drink afterwards. And thought of the Mitre—and you.' He sat back in his chair. 'So. Apart from the angry cousin, is there someone in your life?'

'No. I'm on my own.' She drank some tea to counter a fleeting wave of misery. 'My mother died when I was born.'

Joe reached a hand across the table to grasp hers in sympathy. 'Your father brought you up?'

'No. Relatives.' She detached her hand and got up. 'Time I went home, if that's all right with you.'

He got to his feet. 'I obviously touched a nerve.'

She smiled ruefully. 'Only because I'm a bit on edge after meeting Adam.'

'I'll try to keep off contentious subjects in future,' he promised. 'So, when can I see you again?'

'I work pretty unsociable hours,' Fen reminded him.

He raised a straight dark eyebrow. 'Is that a no?'

'No, it's not. I'm off this Sunday, if that's any good.'

'Sunday it is. What shall we do?'

Not sure how much of Sunday he had in mind, Fen played safe. 'You choose.'

'Let's see what the weather's like and go from there. How soon do you surface after Saturday night at the Mitre?'

'Nine-ish?'

'I'll ring you.' Joe took her hand again, and turned the palm up. Fen stood very still as he bent his head to kiss it. He straightened, and smiled into her watchful eyes, then closed her fingers over the spot his lips had touched and led the way from his elegant apartment.

'I'm afraid we'll have to go back to the Mitre,' Fen told him as he drove off. 'My car's parked there, which is partly why I forced myself on you. I don't want Adam to know which car I drive these days, either.'

'Curiouser and curiouser,' said Joe casually. 'Does Cousin Adam lust after you, by any chance?'

'Absolutely not!' said Fen, turning a shocked face on him. 'He's married, with two children.'

Joe shrugged. 'It doesn't always rule such things out.'

'I know that! But it does in this case. It's not that kind of thing at all.' She heaved a sigh. 'We had a quarrel. Such a bad one I'm still licking my wounds.'

When they reached the deserted Mitre car park Joe switched off the engine and turned to her.

'Now this cousin of yours knows where you work, he'll be back.'

'Yes,' she agreed glumly. 'And from the mood Adam was in tonight I don't think a fond reconciliation is on the cards. No matter. I can handle him.'

'If you say so. Nevertheless, I'll follow you home and see you safely inside your house,' said Joe, with the kind of casual Alpha-male assurance Fen normally objected to. But he came to your rescue again tonight, she reminded herself. Be nice.

Joe walked with her to her car, and waited until she drove off before following her to narrow, treeless Farthing Street, where it was rare to find all the streetlights functioning at the same time. True to form, the one outside her house was still out of action. Fen parked on the square of concrete in front of her house, and waited for Joe to follow her round to the back.

'It's hellish dark out here,' he said, as she opened the door. 'Turn all your lights on. Better still, I'll do it.'

'Joe,' she said tartly. 'I'm perfectly capable of turning them on myself.'

He backed away, hands held up in mock surrender. 'Of course you are. Goodnight, then, Fenella. I'll ring you on Sunday morning.'

'Thanks again for playing along with me tonight.'

'No thanks necessary—I enjoyed it enormously.'

For a moment Fen felt sure he would kiss her, and felt a pang of regret when Joe merely smiled and told her to lock the door behind him.

Fen had been taken on originally for part-time work at the Mitre, but due to staff holidays she'd worked both shifts each day for the past week, with just a short break in the late afternoon. And, though Saturday was always busy, this one was made doubly exhausting by the day-long worry over whether Adam would turn up at some point, hellbent on confrontation.

'Just thank your lucky stars the Mitre isn't residential,' said Jilly, as they tidied up after the lunch-time wave was over. 'A friend of mine works at the Chesterton, and takes a turn at serving breakfast as well.'

'Poor soul! Do one's feet ever get used to it?' groaned Fen.

'Mine haven't. Incidentally, have you heard?' added Jilly, chuckling. 'Diane rang the boss today to say she'll be just fine for her Tuesday gig—surprise, surprise.'

Fen blew out her cheeks in relief. 'Thank heavens for that! I'd planned to collapse with some mysterious complaint if Tim asked me to fill in again.'

Towards the end of a hectic evening Fen began to relax. Adam was not going to barge in and make a scene after all. Instead, just as her feet were telling her it would be really nice to go home, she saw Joe come up to the bar.

She smiled warmly. 'Hi. You're obviously getting a taste for our beer.'

'Or something,' he said, returning the smile. 'Single Scotch and a lot of soda, please.'

Fen provided him with his drink, rang up his money on the register, handed him the change, then moved on to the next customer. It was half an hour before she had any opportunity to speak to Joe. 'Same again?' she asked.

'Better make it a straight soda.'

By this time the bar had quietened down enough for him to ask if she'd had any problems during the day.

'Nothing other than my aching feet.'

'No visitations from angry cousins, then. What time do you get off?'

'In half an hour or so. But don't worry. I won't need a bodyguard tonight.'

He leaned closer to look her in the eye. 'Does that mean you don't want me to follow you home?'

She shrugged, determined not to look too eager. 'You can if you like.'

'Don't overwhelm me with enthusiasm,' he said dryly. 'I'll wait in the corner over there, nursing my drink.'

It seemed a long half-hour. Fen had begun to consider herself reasonably proficient after two weeks in the job. But with a steady dark gaze trained on her at intervals from the far corner of the bar she was all fingers and thumbs as she poured drinks and took money—something noted with huge glee by Jilly, but with less by Tim Mathias when he made his rounds.

'Any problems, Fen? That's the guy who was staring at you when you were singing.'

Her eyebrows rose. 'Really? I thought you meant Adam.'

'No. Adam saw you when he came in to book a meal for next week—'

'Which night is he coming?' she said quickly.

'Tuesday.'

'In that case can I switch shifts?'

'After you helped me out over Diane I can hardly refuse, can I? Time you went home now,' Tim added. 'You too, Jilly.'

In the staffroom Jilly eyed Fen speculatively. 'The bloke who was watching you out there—is he taking you home?'

'Sort of. I drive and he follows behind to make sure I'm safe, that's all. He's the one who came to my rescue the other night when I was mugged.'

'Is he, now? He can rescue me any time he likes,' said Jilly enviously, and sighed. 'Heigh-ho. Time I was off home to the arms of my beloved. If he's still awake by this time.' She paused. 'Look, kid, is this chap on the level? What does he do for a living? Something exciting?'

'He sells insurance,' said Fen, chuckling at Jilly's disappointment.

The sight of Joe Tregenna leaning against her car was so welcome Fen realised she would miss him on the nights when he wasn't waiting for her. Which was idiotic. She didn't need a bodyguard. She wasn't the nervous kind. Just the same, she liked having Joe around. Liked it a lot.

'I've been thinking,' he said, as she joined him.

'About what, in particular?'

'Tomorrow.'

'And?'

'If we make an early enough start, how about making for a beach somewhere?'

'We're a fair distance from any beach.'

'Not the way I drive.'

Fen laughed. 'I don't like the sound of that.'

'I'm careful. You'll be perfectly safe. A couple of hours and we could be stretched out in the sun.'

'In that case, you're on!'

'If it rains we'll think of something else,' Joe said, taking her agreement for granted.

Fen thought about this on the drive to Farthing Street, knowing that with any other man this would be a total turn-off. But with Joe it was different. And the reassurance of his headlights in her driving mirror went a long way to restoring the sense of security she'd taken utterly for granted until recently. She'd sailed confidently through life, certain that bad things happened to other people, never to Fenella Dysart. Not that the episode with a couple of naughty kids could be counted as very desperate. But she could have done without it, just the same. In the circumstances.

When Fen arrived she waited for Joe to park his car. 'Are you coming in?' she asked, as he strolled towards her.

'Only to see you through the door. As I said before, you could do with a light out here.'

'It's better when the streetlight's working.'

'Why isn't it at the moment?'

'No idea.'

'Complain to the council. In the meantime do something about security lights.'

'I only rent the place,' she reminded him, as he followed her inside. 'And for what I pay I doubt the landlord would cough up for such an exotic extra.'

'Couldn't you have found somewhere more

comfortable?' Joe frowned as he took inventory of the cheerless little kitchen. By way of fittings it boasted a couple of cupboards, a small electric cooker, a single-drainer sink, an elderly washing machine, and the brand new microwave Fen had obviously bought herself. 'Not exactly glossy magazine material.'

She shrugged. 'I needed somewhere in a hurry. This was available because it's vacation time. Normally it's a student let.'

'Was the flatshare in a more salubrious part of town?'

'No. In London. What time do you want to start in the morning?'

'I'll check the forecast and give you a ring.'

'Fine. Like some coffee?'

'No, thanks. Now I've made sure you're safe I'll take off and let you get those feet of yours to bed. See you tomorrow.' Joe smiled at her, sketched a salute, then went out, leaving Fen staring, crestfallen, at the door he'd closed behind him.

One thing she had to say for Joe Tregenna: he wasn't asking for a thing in return for his help. As any other male of her acquaintance would have done. Though she would have rather liked a goodnight kiss. She sighed. Maybe he just didn't fancy her.

Oh, well, she thought philosophically, as she turned the key in the lock, it was probably a good thing he hadn't stayed. He wouldn't like the sitting room any better than the kitchen. She didn't either.

She kept her television and video recorder upstairs on the dressing table in the bedroom. Which was marginally more comfortable than the other rooms due to curtains she'd bought ready-made, with matching covers for the bed, a couple of cushions, and the new mattress which had been vital before she could bring herself to sleep there. The bedroom now felt more like her own personal space, which the sitting room, with its hideous wallpaper and imitation leather furniture, never would.

She smiled wryly as she got ready for bed. She'd never been given to mooching in her bedroom all day as a teenager, but these days, with a whole house at her disposal, she led a typical bedsit type of existence.

The phone rang early next morning, startling Fen awake. She stretched out a hand for the cellphone kept charged by the bed, and blinked owlishly as she said a hoarse hello.

'I woke you,' said Joe Tregenna, amused.

'You certainly did.' She yawned, and turned to look at her watch. 'You sadist! It's only just after six.'

'I'll be round in half an hour. The forecast

promised sunshine, so let's make the most of it. See you.'

Fen put the phone back, shaking her head in amused disbelief. The possibility that she might have fancied a lie-in after such a hectic working week had obviously never occurred to him.

After the fastest bath of her life she pulled jeans over a scarlet bikini, added a stretchy striped T-shirt, and managed to gulp down a cup of coffee and twist her hair into a braid before Joe rapped on the kitchen door.

'Good morning!' He smiled, looking so fit and fresh in khakis and white sweatshirt it tired her to look at him. 'How are you this morning?'

'Not human yet. I'm not really an early-morning person,' she warned. 'I'll probably snore in the car. Where *are* we going?'

'Mystery trip. You can guess as we go along. Have you packed swimming gear?'

'Yessir,' she said, saluting. 'Plus sunscreen, hat, sunglasses and cagoule.'

'Have you no faith, woman? The sun's shining out there!'

'For now it is,' Fen said darkly. 'Hang on a minute.' She raced upstairs to collect her cushions, and ran down to find Joe peering into the sitting room.

'Hell, Fen, it's worse than the kitchen,' he said, appalled. 'You actually spend time in here?'

'None at all.' She handed him the cushions and pulled on her denim jacket. 'Let's go.'

In the comfortable leather-scented interior of Joe's car, Fen leaned back with a sigh and relaxed as they threaded through roadworks to make for the motorway.

'Sorry,' she said, yawning. 'I won't be much company for a while.'

'Take a nap. Mind if I play some music?'

'A lullaby would be good.'

While the Jaguar ate up the miles to the strains of Ravel, Fen wriggled comfortably into her nest of cushions and was fast asleep before they'd gone a couple of miles.

'Are we there?' she yawned later, when the car slowed down.

'Not yet—pitstop for coffee,' Joe informed her.

Fen sat up, pushed back a few escaping strands of hair, and smiled at him as he parked in the motorway service station. 'As company on a day out I'm a washout so far,' she said apologetically. 'I swear I'll improve as the day goes on.'

'After double shifts at the Mitre all week no wonder you feel tired. Come on, out you get. We need coffee.'

'Urgently, if I'm to stay awake all the way.' She eyed him challengingly as they walked towards the restaurant. 'Would you have been as keen on the trip if you'd known that I'm such boring company?'

Joe gave the matter due consideration. 'On reflection I think I prefer peaceful silence to incessant chattering.'

'You wait until the journey home,' she said, giggling.

'Do that again!'

'What?'

'The girly little laugh. But first,' he added hastily, as she glared at him, 'tell me what you want and I'll fetch it for you.'

She snatched up a tray. 'No need. I can get my own.'

There was an argument when Joe insisted on paying for her toast and coffee, but in the end Fen gave in rather than provide more entertainment for the girl at the cash register.

'I asked you out, so I foot the bill,' he said flatly, as they sat down by a window.

She buttered her toast, frowning at him. 'Look, Joe, I'm perfectly able to pay my own way.'

He drank some coffee, his eyes gleaming at her through the steam. 'OK. You can pay for lunch.'

Great. It would serve her right if he fancied a three-course meal in some expensive hotel. 'I wasn't being difficult,' she said belatedly, remembering she had good cause to be grateful to him. 'I just like to be independent.'

His smile disarmed her completely. 'No offence taken. But if you're paying for lunch I'll treat you to another coffee.'

'Where *are* we going?' Fen asked, on the way back to the car.

'If you stay awake for the rest of the journey I'll tell you when we're nearly there,' Joe promised.

She gave him a warning look as she fastened her seatbelt. 'Tell me now, or I don't pay for lunch.'

He laughed. 'I never intended you to.'

She ground her teeth in frustration. 'Has anyone ever told you that you're an infuriating man, Joe Tregenna?'

'Frequently, but they invariably succumb to my charm in the end,' he said smugly, and drove off to rejoin the motorway.

CHAPTER THREE

THEIR destination, which Fen guessed once they were driving through the county of Dorset, was Lulworth Cove.

'This is just perfect,' she said, delighted, when they reached the white cobbled beach, which was an idyll in watercolour in the sunshine, with boats riding at anchor on a calm blue sea.

Joe unfolded the steamer chairs he'd taken from the boot of the car, handed Fen into one, then let himself down in the other with a sigh of pleasure. 'I borrowed these from my neighbours in the hope that the weather would stay good,' he said with satisfaction, and glanced at her over his sunglasses. 'Have you been here before?'

'Once, when I was very small, but I don't remember much about it.'

'Was Cousin Adam along on the outing?'

'Probably,' said Fen shortly. She dug in her bag for her sunscreen, smoothed it over the small area of skin exposed, then put on sunglasses and a white cotton sunhat, and leaned back.

There was silence between them for a while, broken only by the calls of seagulls and scraps of conversation drifting on the air as other sunseekers began approaching over the cobbles.

'I don't mean to be stroppy, Joe,' said Fen, after a while. 'But I just don't want to talk about Adam.'

'Then we won't,' he said promptly, and sat up to open the cool-bag he'd brought. 'Fancy a cold drink? Or I can provide apples, peaches and chocolate.'

Fen sat up, impressed. 'You're very organised.'

'Habit. I was brought up in Cornwall. Days on the beach were part of life.'

'Do your people still live there?' she asked, then gave him a wry grin. 'Which is a nerve, I know, when I refuse to discuss my own background.'

'I'm perfectly happy to discuss mine,' he said, lying back in his chair. 'I've got two older brothers. They're London-based. But my parents are still in Cornwall, in the same house on the headland above the village of Polruan, with a path leading down to a small cove.'

'Sounds wonderful.'

'Until I left home I never appreciated how idyllic my childhood actually was. Not a lot of money to spare, but we lacked nothing important. My parents are retired now, but they both taught at the village school.'

'Did you go there, too?'

'All three of us, until we were eleven.'

Fen's eyes sparkled. 'Did it cause trouble with the other kids—because your parents were teachers, I mean?'

Joe grinned. 'It meant quite a few bloody noses after school. My father was the headmaster, and famous for coming down like a ton of bricks on fighting. But he was forced to turn a blind eye in our case, because my mother was adamant that we sorted things for ourselves.'

'So you grew up tough, Joe. No wonder you pitched in when you saw me in a spot of bother.'

'Only because I saw a girl,' he said frankly, and turned to look at her. 'Which was an inspired move, because it led to meeting you.'

'A pretty speech,' she said lightly.

'True, though. Want some chocolate?'

'No, thanks. It might spoil my lunch. Where shall we eat?'

'Right here. On the way down I noticed a place that does crab sandwiches to take out.'

'Perfect!'

As the morning wore on the sun grew hotter, and after a while Joe got up and stripped down to shorts.

'You'd better have some of this,' said Fen, hand-ing him the sunscreen.

He slapped some on his chest and legs, then returned it. 'Could you do my back?'

Fen smoothed the cream over his impressive shoulders, then gave them a tap. 'There. All done.'

'How about you?' asked Joe.

'I'll just take my jacket off.'

Fen had never suffered from shyness, but with Joe for an audience she couldn't bring herself to strip down to the bikini.

'Fen,' said Joe after a while, staring out to sea. 'It strikes me that I was a bit insensitive to ramble on to you about my childhood.'

'Not a bit,' she said cheerfully. 'I liked hearing about it. Tell me more.'

'I probably painted it a bit rosier than it was. The three of us squabbled a lot, and grumbled when required to dig the garden, wash dishes, or walk the dogs. But because my mother worked hard at school as well as at home, my father considered it only fair that the rest of us, including himself, pitched in with the chores. There was no money for hired help, and just coping with the family wash was a major undertaking. The three of us were into rugby, athletics, cricket, and in my case tennis.'

'Which meant mountains of dirty sports gear,' said Fen, feeling sympathy for Mrs Tregenna.

Joe glanced at her. 'In your situation I imagine you had to do your share of chores, too?'

'Some,' she agreed briefly, and pulled her hat low over her eyes.

Eventually Joe got up, thrust his feet into deck shoes and pulled on his shirt. 'I'm hungry. I'll go and hunt up some lunch. You keep off those aching feet of yours, Fen, and stay here with the gear. If there's no crab, what shall I bring?'

'Anything they've got.'

She watched him as he strolled out of sight, then turned back to gaze out over the sea, aware of how much she was enjoying Joe's company. This Melissa of his was mad to refuse the move to Pennington with him. And stupid to assume she could take over his flat rent-free. Joe Tregenna was no one's fool. Even on short acquaintance Fen knew there was steel behind the humour in those navy blue eyes, a combination which grew in appeal each time they met.

Taking advantage of his absence, Fen took off her jeans and shirt and hung them on the back of the chair, then applied a coat of sunscreen to the expanse of skin left bare by the scarlet bikini. There was a small garden behind the house in Farthing Street, not much more than a patch of rough grass with a washing line, separated from the house next door by a high privet hedge. But it gave her a secluded place to lie in the sun for those brief periods when the weather was kind during her time off. So far she'd been lucky with the weather, but the idea of Farthing Street in constant rain was so depressing she refused to think of it.

It was some time before Joe returned with lunch. He swept her a glance of open appreciation, then sat down on the footrest of the deckchair and took packets of sandwiches from a carrier bag, plus some ripe red tomatoes and a clutch of paper napkins. *Madame,*' he said triumphantly, 'lunch is served. Sorry I was so long. The sandwiches are cut fresh to order, and I had to stand in line.'

'Worth waiting for,' Fen assured him. 'But first could you just slap some cream on my back? I've done the rest.'

'Spoilsport,' said Joe, grinning, his touch swift and impersonal over her back and shoulders. 'Right. Now let's eat.'

The sandwiches were generously filled, made with thick slices of crusty bread, the crab seasoned with lemon and black pepper, and Fen bit into one with an ecstatic groan of appreciation. 'Wow, these are amazing!'

Joe nodded, munching. 'As good as the ones they make at the Anchor in Polruan.'

Later, after making inroads on the peaches and chocolate for dessert, they sat in comfortable silence for a while, drowsy with good food and warmth. Eventually, when Joe began to doze, Fen pulled on her shirt and sneakers and went for a stroll. When she got back with two cartons of coffee Joe was sitting up, watching her pick her way over the cobbles.

'You're an angel! Just what I need. I woke up with a fur-lined mouth.'

'Thought you might.' Fen sat down. 'First I'm going to drink this, then I'm going to treat my feet to a spot of thalassotherapy.'

'What the devil's that?'

'Dunking them in seawater,' she said, grinning. 'Want to paddle?'

'I fancy a swim. How about you?'

She shook her head. 'Feet only. The rest of me stays dry.'

Joe took the empty cup from her and stuffed it into the empty sandwich bag with his. Then he took her hand and pulled her up. 'Come on, then.'

As they crunched their way over the cobbles Fen tripped and almost overbalanced, but Joe fielded her neatly, held her close against his sun-warmed chest for an instant, then kept firm hold of her hand until they reached the water.

It was colder than expected, and Fen hopped up and down as the waves lapped over her feet. 'Definitely no swim for me,' she gasped. 'Are you sure about this?'

Joe gave her a scornful look, waded out until it was deep enough, then dived into the water. He emerged yards away, raking wet hair back from his grinning face, and waved. 'You don't know what you're missing!'

'Oh, yes, I do,' she shouted back, and, after a minute or two of watching him power his way through the water, picked her way back over the cobbles to the chairs. She waggled her toes to dry her feet, took off her shirt and applied another layer of sunscreen while Joe made for the beach.

When he stood up, water streaming down the body which had felt so good against hers, she had to admit that Joe Tregenna appealed to her strongly—in every way other than his tendency to take over at times. She watched as he made his way towards her over the cobbles, admiring his broad shoulders and long, muscular legs. These days her most constant problem was loneliness. Which was new in her life. What she needed was a new friend. The girls at the Mitre all had boyfriends or husbands, and in any case worked the same antisocial hours she did. And, if she were honest, Joe was exactly the kind of friend she needed: an attractive, intelligent man willing to accept her just as she was, no background details required.

'That's a very stern expression, Fen,' said Joe, as he joined her. 'Could you fish in my bag for a towel?'

'I bet you're freezing, only you won't admit it,' she teased, tossing it to him.

'It did me the world of good,' he insisted, rubbing himself down. He secured the towel round his hips and searched in his bag. 'This is where you gaze discreetly out to sea!'

Fen chuckled, and pulled her hat over her eyes. 'Use my towel for your hair.'

The rest of the day went quickly. At one point Joe went back to the café to fetch tea, and afterwards they just talked easily, or fell into companionable, comfortable silence. But eventually it grew too cool to sit, and they began to pack up.

'It's been a lovely day,' said Fen, licking the ice-cream cone Joe had bought her on the way back from the beach.

'Is there something pressing you need to get back for tonight?' he asked when they reached his car.

'No. Why?'

He opened the boot to stow the chairs away. 'We could go back across country and find a pub somewhere for dinner.'

'I'm a bit grubby,' said Fen doubtfully, looking down at herself.

'Does it matter?'

'No. No, of course it doesn't.' She smiled at him. 'Though this time I'll be awake all the way, probably talk about myself non-stop, and you'll be glad to get me back to Farthing Street instead of taking me out for a meal.'

Joe shook his head. 'I doubt it. So far I know where you live, and that you work at the Mitre. But otherwise, Miss Dysart, you're very sparing with personal details.'

'Is that a problem for you?'

He gave her a straight look. 'You obviously want it that way, so, no, it isn't.'

'Good.' She took off her sunglasses and smiled at him as she slid into the passenger seat. 'But don't worry. I'm very law-abiding, Joe. No secret criminal dossier. My décor may not be up to yours, but I'm perfectly respectable. Honest!'

He laughed and went round the car to get in. 'You won't nick my silver, then.'

'No. Though I'd like to steal your flat. You've got great taste.'

His lips twitched as he switched on the ignition. 'Confession time. I bought the place from a couple who were moving to a place in the Mediterranean sun, and some of their furniture was included in the sale.'

'You mean none of that is yours?'

'I bought the teapot and mugs myself! But once the flat in London is sold I'll transfer my own stuff up here. Though I'll need a dining table and chairs for the other half of the main room, which looks a bit empty as it is.'

'Not to me,' Fen assured him. 'Just wonderfully uncluttered after Farthing Street.'

'If you dislike it why do you live there?'

Why, indeed? She shrugged. 'I told you. It was *very* cheap.'

'I should damn well hope so. The furniture in that sitting room is gross.' He took a hand from the wheel and touched hers in apology. 'Sorry. But surely other people agree with me?'

'You're the only visitor I've had.'

There was silence after this statement, while Joe concentrated on the Sunday evening traffic. 'Why me, then?' he said eventually.

'Because you happened along on your rescue mission.' Her chin lifted. 'I only asked you in that night because I was a bit shaken after my encounter with Robbie.'

'Thanks!' He slanted a look at her. 'But why no one else?'

'I'm in my Garbo phase,' she returned flippantly.

Joe decided to press on as far as he could before stopping for dinner, but when they found a place which appealed to them they were told lunch was the only meal served on Sundays.

'That could be a problem in other places, especially at this time of night,' said Fen. 'How about we pick up a Chinese and eat it on my kitchen table?'

'Done. We'll postpone the *haute cuisine* until another night,' he said promptly.

She shook her head at him, laughing.

'What?' he demanded, as they got back in the car.

'It's the way you just assume I'll fall in with whatever you suggest.'

He shrugged. 'Only dinner.'

'True. Let's go. I'm hungry! In fact,' she added, searching in her bag, 'I've got a flyer here from the Chinese restaurant nearest to my place, so I could order now.'

Joe eyed her in admiration. 'Clever girl!'

'Hunger fuels the thought processes—how long before we get there?' Fen consulted him on his preferences, used his cellphone to place the order, then sat back, smiling at him. 'All this is a big improvement on last Sunday, Joe Tregenna.'

'What did you do?'

'I worked all day. And the week before that it rained so I went to the cinema.'

'Alone?'

'Yes.'

Again he put out a hand to touch hers. 'In future, any time you want company, just say the word.'

Which was why she'd brought the subject up.

Soon afterwards they were back in Farthing Street, digging into the containers spread out on Fen's kitchen table.

'I like to see a woman eat,' approved Joe later, as they scraped the dishes clean.

'It was all that sea air,' said Fen, scrubbing at her mouth with a napkin. 'But if I felt grubby before I feel mega-scruffy now.'

'Whereas to me you look so good all flushed and shiny that I could eat you for dessert,' said Joe conversationally.

She stared so blankly at him he threw back his head and laughed.

'Could I scrub some of this grease off in your bathroom?' he asked unsteadily.

Fen nodded. 'Upstairs, first door you come to.'

When he'd gone off, whistling, she gathered the foil dishes into a bag and put it outside in the bin, feeling outrageously pleased by his remark, and washed her own hands and face under the tap in the sink before Joe came down again. In case he acted on his words.

'The bathroom lives up to the rest of the décor—well, most of it.' He smiled. 'But your bedroom's better.'

Fen's eyes turned to green ice. 'You actually looked in my *bedroom*?'

He nodded, unrepentant. 'I was curious. And if my remark just now had you thinking I was going to jump on you as payment for taking you out for the day, you're wrong. Though as a compliment I meant it,' he added honestly. 'I don't know what's going on in your life, and because you obviously don't want me to know I won't ask. But I can't be the first man to find you attractive.'

'No, you're not,' she agreed. 'Men often say that kind of thing. It's what blokes do, so I took no notice. The angry bit is because my bedroom is my own private space, and strictly off limits.' She looked him in the eye. 'To everyone.'

He returned the look, unmoved. 'It just worried me to think of you sleeping in a room like the one downstairs.'

'And now you're reassured that I've imported a few girly touches to make a little nest you can go home a happy man—how sweet,' she said with sarcasm. 'Thank you for the trip, Joe. Goodnight.'

He stood staring down at her, no trace of humour in his eyes. 'And goodbye? In that case—' He seized her by the shoulders and planted a hot, hard kiss on her mouth, then before she'd gathered her wits pulled her into his arms to kiss her again, enfolding her in an aura of sun-warmed male mixed with her own soap, his lips and tongue seeking, and receiving, a response she couldn't keep back.

Joe smiled as he released her, the laughter back in his eyes. 'You kissed me back.'

'You took me by surprise,' said Fen, sounding so childish, even to her own ears, she gave a snort of laughter.

'That's better,' he said in approval. 'Look, Fen, I didn't go in your bedroom. I just took a quick look through the door in the hope of finding one half-way comfortable room in this grim little house.'

'OK. Sorry I ripped at you.' She shrugged. 'I couldn't do much about the actual bedroom furniture, but the rest is my own. Though it beats me why it matters to you.' But she was hopeful. 'You needn't lose sleep over me, Joe. I'm fine.'

He looked unconvinced. 'Just the same, Fen, will you promise me something?'

'It depends.'

'If you need me any time, just ring. I can be here in minutes.'

She frowned. 'Why do you think I should need you?'

'I don't know. I just have an uneasy feeling about this place. What are your neighbours like?'

'No idea.'

'You see what I mean?'

'No, I don't, so stop it, Joe,' she said irritably, 'you're giving me the creeps.'

But he wasn't listening. 'Fen,' he said after a moment. 'How much do you earn at the Mitre?'

When she told him his eyebrows shot to his hair. 'As little as that? In that case, if I knew of a job which would pay more—enough to let you rent something better than this—would you consider it?'

She shook her head. 'That's very nice of you, Joe, but I really like working at the Mitre.'

'This job would be easier on your feet,' he said, smiling.

Fen couldn't help smiling back. 'A tempting prospect, but no, thanks—' She broke off, startled, as the doorbell rang.

'A visitor at this hour?' said Joe.

'Never had one before. Certainly not at the front door. It opens into the sitting room, so I keep it locked—and bolted.'

'Shall I get it?'

'Of course not; it's my door.' Fen squared her shoulders. 'Probably someone selling something.' The bell rang again, and this time her caller kept a peremptory finger on it. She wrenched back the bolts and opened the door as far as the safety chain allowed. Then stiffened, her eyes hostile at the sight of her visitor.

'Go away,' she snapped, and tried to shut the door. But Adam Dysart stuck a long foot into the aperture and, angry though she was, Fen couldn't bring herself to slam the door on it.

'For God's sake, Fenny,' Adam said impatiently, eyeing what he could see of the room with incredulous distaste. 'We need to talk. Will you stop behaving like a spoilt brat and listen to me?'

'Problems, Fen?' said Joe, coming up behind

her. He slid a protective arm round her waist and held her close.

Adam's jaw clenched, and suddenly Fen realised what kind of impression they were making. Joe was as dishevelled and untidy as she was from the day in the sun and wind, and due to the delay, she realised, exulting, Adam probably thought they'd had to get dressed to come to the door.

'Nothing important, darling,' she assured Joe, and felt his arm tighten. 'Adam isn't staying.'

A statement which took Adam Dysart so much by surprise she was able to slam the door in his face, then ram the bolts home to make sure he got the message.

When the doorbell remained silent afterwards Fen's eyes filled, and Joe took her hand to lead her back to the kitchen, then held her close in his arms.

'Don't cry,' he said into her hair. 'And I won't ask. Though I can't help wondering why you hate this cousin of yours so much.'

'You've got it wrong.' Fen drew away, pushing a lock of hair back from her tear-stained face. 'I don't hate Adam. I love him very much.'

Joe stared at her narrowly for a moment, then shook his head. 'Getting to know you, Fenella Dysart, is like trying to piece one of those huge jigsaw puzzles together.'

She sat down at the table again. 'I told you. Adam and I had a row.'

Joe leaned against the cooker, looking down at her. 'A major battle, obviously.'

'Yes.' She gave him a wicked little smile. 'Actually, I'm glad Adam's seen where I live.'

'Even though he's likely to come ringing your doorbell again?'

'I won't open the door next time.'

He raised an eyebrow. 'What happens if *I* come knocking at your door?'

Fen gave him a glinting look. 'We'll have to think up a special knock so I know it's you.'

Joe pulled her up from her chair. 'So it isn't goodbye, then?'

'God heavens, no,' she said flippantly. 'You're *much* too useful to me.'

'Am I now?' he said softly. 'Then perhaps I should mention that my services don't come free.'

'You mean I won't be able to afford them?' she said, short of breath.

'Just a kiss or two,' he said affably.

'Sounds reasonable.'

Joe bent his head and kissed her, and this time Fen made no attempt to control her response. 'There,' he said huskily, 'that wasn't so bad, was it?'

She shook her head. 'Not bad at all. Talking of

which, I suppose you realise that Adam thought we'd just got out of bed?'

'The thought did cross my mind.' He trailed a finger down her cheek. 'My motive was to let him know you had protection. And make it convincing.'

'You'd better not make it too convincing or you'll have Adam on *your* case too, banging on about your intentions,' she warned, laughing.

'Judging by the look he turned on me,' said Joe, eyes gleaming, 'he's jumped to conclusions about those already.' He paused, looking down at her. 'Adam calls you Fenny.'

Her smile died abruptly. 'Yes. But I don't answer to that any more.'

'Why not?'

'Fenny had to grow up.'

CHAPTER FOUR

WHEN Fen arrived at the Mitre for her single evening shift next day Tim Mathias called her into his office, shut the door and told her to sit down.

'Something wrong?' she asked uneasily.

He nodded. 'Look, Fen, I'm really sorry about this, but I'm going to have to let you go.'

'Let me go?' She stared at him in dismay. 'You mean—you're firing me?'

'Afraid so.'

'Is my work unsatisfactory, then?'

'No, far from it.'

'Then why?'

'Adam asked me to,' he informed her reluctantly. 'I should have told you when you finished your Saturday shift, but Grace wouldn't hear of it.'

Fen fought for calm. 'That's very sweet of her. Does she think my job here is none of Adam's business?'

'Yes. But it's very much mine,' said Tim firmly. 'Adam's a good friend. And he's hellish worried about you. I can see his point of view, Fen. Which is why I can't keep you on. He wants you back.'

'That's not going to happen, Tim,' she informed him as Grace Mathias burst in, looking daggers at her husband.

'I still say Fen stays, Tim. She's a damn good worker, and the customers like her.'

'But, darling, we spent our entire Sunday arguing about this. You know I gave Adam my word,' said Tim stubbornly.

'And I think you should have stood firm. Fen did you a favour by stepping in for Diane, remember.'

'I know, I know. But that's the point. It was Fen's turn with Martin that caused the trouble.'

Grace looked her husband in the eye. 'I like Adam just as much as you do, Tim Mathias, but who we hire and fire is up to us.'

Fen held up a hand. 'It's very good of you to fight my corner, Grace, but I draw the line at coming between husband and wife.' She gave Tim a tight little smile. 'Don't worry. I'll go quietly. But I'm sorry I can't stay. I liked working here.'

'And we liked having you,' he said, openly relieved she was taking it well. 'If I'd had any idea how Adam would react I wouldn't have asked you to sing. He's known you were working here from the first, of course—'

'What?' Fen stared at him, transfixed. 'You mean he's known all along?'

'Yes, of course. I wouldn't have taken you on otherwise.'

'I see. At least I do now.' She smiled brightly. 'Goodbye, then. Thanks for having me for a while.'

'You could stay until you find something else, at least, Fen,' said Grace, looking worried.

Fen hesitated, then shook her head. 'Better I go right away, with Adam on the warpath.'

'Then Tim will pay you two weeks' money at double shift rate,' Grace said firmly.

And minutes later, after a surprisingly emotional leavetaking from Jilly and the rest of the staff, Fen was on her way back to Farthing Street.

She spent an angry, miserable evening camped out in the bedroom, heaping curses on Adam Dysart's head, not only for getting her fired, but because he'd known she was at the Mitre all along. Fen seethed as she searched through the local newspaper for a suitable job. Or, better still, a really *un*suitable job Adam wouldn't approve of at all, maybe in some club where dancers twined themselves round poles. Though if there were places in Pennington like that she'd never heard of them.

Fen's sense of humour got the better of her at that point, and she laughed out loud. Then heaved an irritable sigh. It was her own fault for targeting the Mitre for a job. She'd been given one there because Tim knew Adam, only to be turfed out again the minute Adam cracked the whip. The power of the old school tie, she thought bitterly.

Fen's spirits rocketed when she heard rapping on the kitchen door later, in the code Joe had devised the night before. She abandoned the sandwich she was making and ran to let him in, smiling at him in such radiant welcome his eyes widened in surprise.

'Am I glad to see you,' she said, taking his hand to pull him inside.

'So I see,' said Joe, smiling, then frowned. 'And don't imagine I'm not happy about it, but what the hell's going on, Fen? Your friend Jilly told me you aren't working at the Mitre anymore—she sent her love, by the way.'

'That's nice. They're a great bunch there—I'll miss them.' Her eyes gave off angry green sparks. 'I was sacked.'

'Good God—why?'

'Adam told Tim to get rid of me.'

Joe's eyes sharpened. 'And Mathias did, just like that?'

Fen nodded. 'Grace was all for my staying on, but rather than cause trouble between them I accepted my wages, made my farewells, and bought the local paper on the way home to look through "Situations Vacant".'

'Are you going to let this cousin of yours get away with it?' demanded Joe. 'The Mitre's a respectable outfit. What did he have against your working there?'

'Nothing, apparently. Unknown to me he'd given Tim the Dysart seal of approval about the bar work from the beginning.' She made a face. 'It was my party piece that did the damage. You saw his reaction to that first-hand.'

'I certainly did.' Joe looked at her sandwich. 'I'm interrupting your supper.'

'I'm glad you are! I bought some beer today. Would you like one?'

'As long as you don't ask me to drink it in that appalling room next door!'

Fen looked at him for a moment, then shrugged. 'All right. Come up to my bedroom, then.'

'I meant,' he said, looking down his nose, 'that I'd rather sit here at the kitchen table.'

'Oh. Sorry!' She bit her lip, eyeing him in appeal. 'Look, Joe, don't you be angry with me, too. I'm in need of a friend right now.'

Joe poured some beer into the glass she gave him, looking at her thoughtfully. 'You know, Fen, it's hard to believe you don't have any friends at all.'

'Of course I do.' She heaved a sigh. 'My best

friend, Laura, works in London. Other school-friends have married, or moved away, and the people I met in college are scattered far and wide. So right now, here in Pennington, I'm on my own.'

'But is Adam your only relative?'

'No.' She abandoned the sandwich and drank some coffee, eyeing his full glass. 'Did I buy the wrong brand of beer?'

'This is fine.' Joe drank some of it, then stretched a hand across the table to take hers. 'So, Fenella Dysart, speaking as a friend, what do you plan to do now?'

'Look for another job.'

'How about qualifications?'

She shrugged. 'Quite good exam results in school. Business Studies in college.'

'In which case, I take it the job at the Mitre was purely a stopgap until you found something better.'

'And to annoy Adam,' she admitted candidly. 'Though I needn't have bothered. It only worked when he caught me doing the gig.'

Joe eyed her speculatively. 'Any work experience before the Mitre?'

'Why are you asking?'

'Because Safehouse Insurance—the outfit I work for—is taking on more staff. It employs far more women than men, so you'd be in with a good chance.'

She brightened. 'Doing what, exactly?'

'Taking calls from customers with domestic emergencies and sorting out their insurance problems.'

'Is that what you do?' she said, surprised.

'Yes.' He smiled, and released her hand. 'The salary's not astronomical, but it's a hell of a sight better than your earnings at the Mitre.' He took his wallet from his back pocket and fished out a card. 'You'll see the advertisement in the paper soon.'

'Thank you.' Fen secured the card to the fridge with a magnet. 'You said women, plural, so obviously the firm employs a fair number of people?'

He nodded. 'It's the new building on Oxford Road. It's a good outfit to work for. There's a subsidised canteen, and once the new branch is up and running there'll be a share scheme for the staff, team activities, parties, and so on.'

'Sounds great.' Fen eyed him questioningly. 'But would you really want me working in the same place as you?'

He grinned. 'It's a big building. I could probably hack it.'

'Then, thank you. I'll watch for the ad.'

'But until then,' said Joe soberly, 'tell me the truth, Fen. Can you manage financially?'

'Yes, I can,' she said, touched. 'But thank you for asking.'

'If you get the job I suggest the first thing you do is move,' he said, looking round him with distaste.

'I need the job first. Pity it's such a respectable one, though.' Eyes dancing, she told him about the pole-dancing fantasy.

But Joe was appalled. 'Dammit, Fen, if you'd even think of going that far to annoy your cousin what the hell was your fight about?'

'Hey, I was joking,' she said, astonished. 'Even if there are places like that in Pennington, I literally don't measure up for the job!'

Joe jumped to his feet and pulled her up and into his arms, holding her so tightly she panicked.

'Stop it! Let me go.'

His arms slackened slightly but his eyes bored relentlessly into hers. 'If you wore yesterday's bikini to audition, Fen, believe me, you'd be hired on the spot.'

'I was *joking*,' she repeated, and blinked fiercely. 'My, my, what a nice day I've had. First I get sacked, then I get ripped at by you to top it off.' Angry tears welled up in her eyes.

'Don't!' Joe pressed her against his chest, his cheek on her hair. 'Don't cry, Fen. Please.' He gave a bitter little laugh. 'But you know exactly which buttons to push. I can almost sympathise with Adam.'

Fen shoved him away, and snatched a sheet of kitchen paper from the roll by the cooker, but Joe recaptured her.

'I know a better way to dry tears,' he said, smiling down at her, and began licking them away. And instead of objecting, Fen gave an unsteady laugh.

'My dog used to do that,' she said huskily, then burst into tears again. This time Joe sat down on one of the kitchen chairs and pulled her on his lap, holding her close until the storm was over.

'Sorry,' she said thickly, and sat upright. 'Shouldn't have mentioned the dog.'

'What breed?'

'Retriever.'

'These relatives of yours let you have a pet, then?'

Fen slid off his lap and turned away for more kitchen paper. 'Yes.'

Joe got to his feet. 'Right. How about making a date for that dinner we didn't have last night? Tomorrow?'

She spun round, reddened eyes shining. 'Yes, *please*, Joe. May I choose the place?'

'Of course. I'm the stranger in town. Where do you want to go?'

'The Mitre.'

Joe looked taken aback. 'Are you sure about that?'

'The food's good.'

'And you quite fancy showing your ex-boss that you're on top of the world even if he did sack you,' he said dryly.

She gave him a triumphant smile. 'Got it in one. But we can eat somewhere else if you like.'

'Come off it, Fenella Dysart, don't even try to do meek,' he said, laughing. 'I'll ring the Mitre in the morning.'

'Thanks a lot, Joe.' She planted a kiss on his cheek in gratitude.

'I want more than that.' He tapped a finger to his lips. 'Right here.'

Fen chuckled as she stood on tiptoe to kiss him.

'What's the joke?' he demanded.

'I so rarely have to do that. Reach up, I mean. I'm lucky if the men I meet are my own height, let alone taller.'

His arms tightened round her. 'So I've got one thing going for me, at least.'

She smiled into the intent eyes inches above hers. 'You've got a whole lot of things going for you, Joe Tregenna!'

'Infuriating and overbearing though I am?'

'Even so.'

'I said you'd succumb to my charm in the end,' he said lightly, and kissed her.

Fen's response, born of tears and the mixed emotions of the day, was intended as gratitude, but the instant their lips met the kiss turned hot and frantic. Joe's hands slid up beneath her shirt, and she gave a shivery little moan that did such damage to his self-control he hung on to it by grasping her shoulders to hold her away from him.

'Is that what you mean by succumbing to your charm?' said Fen, in a gruff, unsteady voice so unlike her own she blinked in surprise and cleared her throat.

'Not exactly!'

'You don't have to hold me off,' she assured him. 'I won't jump on you.'

'The idea is so *I* don't jump on *you*.' Joe heaved in a deep breath and dropped his hands, a wry grin curving his mouth. 'A good thing we're in this hellhole of a kitchen.'

'Don't be so rude about my home, Mr Tregenna!'

'But this isn't your home, is it? And as a setting for seduction this room has serious drawbacks,' he added bluntly.

'Is that what you were going to do? Seduce me?'

'No.' His smile accelerated her pulse-rate. 'I just wanted—still want—to make love to you.'

It was what Fen wanted, too, and by the gleam in Joe's eyes he knew it.

'If I get this job you told me about, I'll move,' she promised huskily.

'Then I'll put in a good word.'

'How did I ever manage to live my life before you came on the scene?' she mocked.

Joe gave a disparaging look round the kitchen. 'Damned if I know.' He cupped her face in his hands and kissed her forehead. 'Sleep well. I'll come for you tomorrow.'

Fen locked up behind him and went to her bedroom, feeling far more pleased with life than she would have believed possible earlier on. Which, she acknowledged with gratitude, was all down to Joe Tregenna, who appeared to look on watching over her as his mission in life. He was no slow-coach when it came to lovemaking, either. Just as well they had been in her kitchen, she thought, not without regret.

Next morning Fen drove out of town and went for a run along the river, her long legs covering the ground less easily at first than they had in the past. At one time a regular run had been part of her life. But the demands on her feet had put a stop to that once she began work at the Mitre. After getting into her stride Fen ran steadily along the towpath for a couple of miles, then upped her speed on the return to the car and drove back to Farthing Street with her face glowing and all her endorphins alive and kicking.

Later she spent an inordinately long time in getting ready, determined to look her best. And in her own personal style this time, which was very different from the effect achieved to fill in for Diane. Instead of a dress she wore a plain black linen trouser suit, its severity softened by a glimpse of flower-splashed apricot chiffon camisole. She slid her bare feet into spike-heeled, strappy black sandals, used a bare minimum of make-up, then piled her glossy hair up on top of her head, teased out a few strands to snake down one side of her face, threaded gold hoops through her earlobes, and ran down when she heard the familiar tattoo on the door.

When she let Joe in his silence was compliment enough. His eyes moved over her with slow, relishing deliberation before he very carefully kissed her on both cheeks. 'Remember my remark about dessert the other night? My statement stands.'

'Thank you,' she said, her smile demure. 'You look good, too.'

Joe wore a lightweight suit which, by the fit across his formidable shoulders, had been custom-made for him. 'I wasn't sure about the dress code in the Mitre restaurant,' he said, putting a package on the table.

'If we look too grand we just take our jack-ets off,' she said, eyeing the package. 'Is that a present?'

'Not really. You can open it when we get back.'

'Can't I open it now?'

'No. I'm hungry.'

When they arrived at the Mitre butterflies fluttered under Fen's black jacket when Tim Mathias greeted them on the way in.

'Hi, Tim,' she said brightly. 'This is Joe Tregenna. We're eating here tonight, so I hope the chef's on form.'

Tim shook Joe's hand and exchanged a few conventional words, but the look he gave Fen spoke volumes.

'Your ex-boss looked like a man with something to say,' commented Jack, as he followed Fen to the restaurant bar.

'Probably wanted to apologise again for sacking me.' She smiled warmly as Grace Mathias came to hand out menus.

There were more introductions, and a gleam of approval for Fen in Grace's keen blue eyes. 'Good to see you. I'll send a waitress over for your order.'

'Grace still feels sorry about letting me go,' said Fen afterwards.

'Nice lady.' Joe leaned back in his chair. 'So how does it feel to return in triumph?'

'Wonderful!'

He smiled at her indulgently. 'What have you been doing with yourself today?'

'Running.'

'Really? Where?'

'I drove a mile or so out of town to a favourite spot of mine. Before working at the Mitre I did that a lot.'

Joe's eyes held hers. 'Perhaps one day you'll tell me what else you did back then. Before the Mitre. That little number you're wearing wasn't bought with money you earned here. So you obviously had a job in London.'

'No. I had a job right here in Pennington.'

'Don't tell me you got fired from that one, too!'

'No. I resigned.'

'Why?'

'Differences with my employer.' Fen studied him over the rim of her glass. 'Does this change your mind about putting a good word in for me with your outfit?'

'Not unless the ex-employer withholds a reference.'

She stared at him, arrested, then shook her head. 'He wouldn't do that—I hope. You said you were hungry. Let's choose.'

There was still no sign of Adam by the time they were shown to a corner table, but Fen was careful to choose a chair which gave her a view of the room and left Joe with his back to it.

The waitress handed him a bottle of wine, winking at Fen. 'Mrs Mathias asks you to accept this with her compliments.'

'I'm getting off very lightly expense-wise tonight,' remarked Joe, over the fettucine they'd chosen for the first course.

'It's very sweet of Grace,' said Fen. 'She made Tim pay me for two weeks of double shifts, too.'

'He must be a very old friend of Adam's to sack you on his instruction, just like that.'

'I suppose I should have expected it after Adam blew his top about the gig. Tim was in school with him, which is why he gave me the job. And in the end why he sacked me. Adam objected, so out goes Fen.' She smiled philosophically. 'Let's talk about something else.'

Joe promptly switched the subject to his London flat, which had found a buyer. 'It means I can move my things up here now.' He surveyed her glowing face. 'Are you flushed with triumph, Fen, or are you too warm?'

'A bit of both,' she said, laughing, and fanned herself with her napkin. 'Mind if I take off my jacket?'

Joe got up to help her, his eyes lingering on the

bare brown shoulders revealed by the filmy top. 'Nice,' he said briefly.

The meal was excellent, but the moment Adam arrived Fen felt too hot and edgy to do justice to it. Though he hadn't noticed her. Or if he had he was ignoring her.

'You're not eating much,' remarked Joe, after the waiter removed the plates from their main course. 'Have some pudding.'

'No, thanks. It's too hot.' She smiled at him. 'Let's have coffee in the little restaurant bar.'

And once they were settled there, thought Fen with satisfaction, Adam would pass them on his way out and confrontation would be unavoidable. She sat back, trying to relax, on the sofa shared with Joe in the bar, but refused the brandy he offered with coffee. 'No, thanks, not after two glasses of wine.'

'Why? Are you likely to get up and dance on the table?'

She laughed. 'No—my career in show business began and ended last week.'

Joe moved closer and took her hand. 'Pity. I enjoyed the way you put those songs over. Though I'm amazed that someone your age is familiar with them.'

'I cheated a bit. I jotted the lyrics down on a bit of paper and hid it on top of the piano. I wasn't so familiar with the second set, so I sat on the piano to sneak a look if I forgot them. But I had no problem with the actual melodies, because my—my relatives were very keen on that kind of thing.'

'Speak of the devil,' said Joe softly. 'One of them's coming our way right now.'

'So he is,' said Fen, smiling in challenge when Adam emerged from the dining room with his companions. She met his eyes, bracing herself for a scene, but to her frustration Adam merely gave her a cool nod and passed her by without a word.

CHAPTER FIVE

FEN glared in disbelief at Adam's retreating back. How dared he ignore her?

'Come on,' said Joe, getting up. 'Let's go.'

She seethed in tight-lipped silence as he helped her into her jacket, waited while he paid the bill, then shook her head impatiently when he asked if she wanted a word with anyone before she left.

'I just want to go home,' she snapped, so furious with Adam she didn't notice at first that Joe was driving in the opposite direction from Farthing Street. 'I meant my place!'

'Too bad,' said Joe flatly. 'You're coiled tight as a spring—you need to unwind. And I refuse to sit in that kitchen of yours tonight, so we'll relax on one of my nice, comfortable sofas instead until you've calmed down.'

'I *am* calm.'

'Like hell you are—more like a volcano about to erupt,' he retorted, ignoring the killing look she threw at him.

'Sit down,' he ordered, when they arrived in the flat. 'What would you like to drink?'

'I don't *want* anything,' Fen said rudely, shrugging out of her jacket.

'Then excuse me while I fetch something for myself.'

After Joe left her alone it took superhuman effort to keep from curling up in a ball to cry her eyes out. Instead Fen took deep, calming breaths while she meticulously folded her jacket before laying it neatly on the other sofa. She smoothed her hair, and by the time Joe returned with a tray she had herself in hand again.

'I'll have to put this on the floor.' He laid it down near her feet. 'The sooner I get the tables and the rest of my gear the better. I've brought mineral water and beer. Can I change your mind about a drink?'

'Yes—water, please.' Fen gave him a wry, shame-faced grin. 'Sorry I snapped your head off. I haven't even thanked you for dinner.'

'No point, when you ate so little of it.' Joe handed her a glass, then sat beside her with his beer. 'The evening didn't pan out quite as you expected, did it?'

She lifted her chin. 'What do you mean?'

He gave her a scathing look. 'Come off it, Fen. You fancied a dramatic little meeting with your cousin at the Mitre, so you set me up for it. You

were like a cat on hot bricks all through the meal.
But Adam didn't play the hand you dealt, did
he?'

Fen's fingers tightened perilously on the glass.
'No. He didn't.'

'Yet you told me you love him,' Joe reminded
her. 'So why are you doing your damnedest to
cause him grief?'

'He's doing the same with me. Not that it's any
of your business,' she retorted.

'If you involve me to get at your cousin it's very
much my business!' There was no humour at all in
the eyes which locked on to hers. 'I strongly object
to being taken for a fool, by Melissa or anyone
else—including you, Fenella Dysart.'

She shrugged carelessly to hide the wound
his words dealt her. 'No big deal, Joe. All I did
was choose the Mitre when you asked me out to
dinner.'

'Because you knew Adam would be there?'

'Yes, I did. And I wanted to show him that getting Tim to fire me hadn't worked.'

'Couldn't you have let me in on the plan?'

'I knew you'd disapprove. Which you do.' She
gave a bitter little laugh. 'Anyway, it all backfired
on me. I've alienated you, and Adam obviously
couldn't care less about me any more.'

'Or maybe he just didn't want a scene in front of

the men with him. It looked like a business dinner to me. What does your cousin do?'

'He runs Dysart's Auction House. It's been in the family for generations. My—my uncle, Adam's father, retired recently and left him in sole charge. Adam's quite well known in the antiques world, especially in fine art. The men with him were probably in the same line of work.' Her eyes flashed coldly. 'Which was no reason for him to ignore me.'

'On Sunday night,' Joe reminded her, 'you slammed your door in his face and told him to get lost. Maybe he's just following your instructions.'

A thought which had already occurred to her. 'If he is I can hardly complain, then, can I?' She finished her glass of water and put it down on the tray. 'Thank you. If you'll call a cab I'll go home and leave you in peace.'

'I don't want you to go home,' he said, surprising her. 'Or to be more specific I hate the thought of your going back to that house. These relatives who brought you up, did they live in Pennington?'

'No.'

'But Adam does?'

'No.'

'In other words, shut up, Tregenna,' he said wearily, and got to his feet. 'No need for a cab. I'll drive you.'

Fen jumped up with such alacrity she stumbled, and Joe's arms shot out to steady her.

'Did you hurt your ankle?' he demanded, and set her back on the sofa. 'Show me.'

She held out a long, narrow foot with pink-painted toenails peeping from the web of flimsy straps attached to a high, slender heel. 'It's fine. My poor old feet are out of practice in fancy shoes, that's all.'

'So why did you wear them?'

'Vanity. Though I don't very often, because they make me so tall.' She smiled wryly. 'I try not to tower over any man brave enough to take me out.'

He grinned as he swung her legs up on the sofa. 'Put those famous feet up there for a while.'

Fen did as he said, rested her head on one of the suede cushions, and wished she could stay there for the foreseeable future. She'd rented the Farthing Street house because it suited her purpose, but she was no more enamoured of it than Joe. 'Thank you. Are you still angry I conned you into the trip to the Mitre tonight?'

'No.' Joe smiled at her. 'Scoot over a bit.'

He sat down in the corner she'd vacated, then to her surprise pulled her onto his lap and sat back, smoothing her head against his shoulder. 'Right then, Orphan Annie, is that comfortable?'

'Yes, very.' She smiled up at him. 'You know,

my real reason for renting such a ghastly house was to make Adam sorry when he saw it.'

'Sorry for you?'

'No. For the horrible things he flung at me during our row.'

Joe looked down at her thoughtfully. 'How long is it since you had the quarrel?'

'Three weeks.' She heaved a sigh. 'It seems like for ever.'

'And your other relatives? Are they taking sides?'

'I don't think any of them can know about it yet. Except Gabriel.'

'Who's he?'

'She. Adam's wife.'

'You say it's none of my business—though somehow it's hard to get that through my head— but it's obvious that this break-up is tearing you apart, Fen. I don't think it's doing Adam much good, either.'

Her lower lip trembled. 'He didn't seem bothered tonight.'

'Perhaps he's given up on you,' said Joe, his arm tightening when her eyes filled. 'Don't cry.'

'Can't you see I'm trying not to?' she said crossly, sniffing hard. 'I've got some tissues in my bag.'

Joe found them, then mopped her face. 'You

look like a panda,' he informed her, and held a tissue to her mouth. 'Spit.'

Fen laughed unsteadily, then held still as he wiped the mascara stains away. 'I'm sorry, Joe,' she said abruptly.

'For what, exactly?'

'For not telling you Adam would be there tonight.'

'Apology accepted.' Joe shifted her more comfortably on his lap. 'Though I think you're playing with fire by making him so angry with you. He's obviously the explosive type.'

She shook her head forlornly. 'Actually, he's not. That's what makes it all so unbearable. Adam's usually even-tempered, and very affectionate. He's a great husband and father—' She gulped. 'But I'm not going to talk about the children or I'll start howling again.'

'He obviously said things during this quarrel that you can't forgive?'

'Yes.'

'Did you retaliate in kind?'

'Of course I did. You saw me lashing out at those silly kids the other night. I was the same with Adam, but with words instead of fists.' Her mouth drooped. 'I'm a real sweetheart when I lose my temper.'

'At least you can admit it. Can't you just go back

to Adam and apologise for the things you said so you can kiss and make up?'

'It's not as simple as that,' she said sadly.

'Nothing ever is.' Joe turned her face up to his. 'So, how about you kiss and make up with me instead?'

'But we haven't quarrelled.'

'Not yet, but give it time,' he said, grinning. 'So let's get the kissing part in first.'

Fen gave a breathless little laugh. 'You're very good for me, Joe Tregenna. It may not seem like it, but I really am grateful to you.'

His eyes darkened. 'I don't want your gratitude, Fenella Dysart.'

Her face fell. 'You mean you want sex?'

To her utter dismay she suddenly found herself thrust to the opposite end of the sofa, watching as Joe strode to the window to stare down at the square, his impressive back eloquent with distaste.

Fen sighed despondently. So much for having Joe Tregenna as a friend.

'I pushed the wrong button again,' she said after a while.

He turned, hands thrust in his pockets, and gazed at her, eyelids at half mast. 'Is sex what you expect men to want from you, Fen?'

She lifted a shoulder. 'It's what it often boils down to, yes.'

'It's not long since we met,' he said tightly, 'but I thought you knew me better than that. I brought you back here tonight for the simple reason that it's bloody uncomfortable in your place, not because I expect payback for a meal you didn't eat. I don't want *sex*.' His eyes blazed into hers. 'But I plead guilty to wanting to make love to you. Haven't you learned the difference yet?'

'Obviously not,' she said, depressed, wondering what would happen if she asked him to teach her. Probably a bad idea in his present mood. She looked at her watch and smiled brightly. 'Time I went. Could you call a taxi for me, please.'

'I said I'll drive you.' He came away from the window. 'Is the foot all right?'

'Fine. But I'll dispense with the heels to go down those stairs.'

'Right. In that case I'd better carry you down—'

'You will not! I'm too heavy.'

Joe gave her another of his all-encompassing looks. 'I've carried heavier weights than you, Fen.'

'Possibly. But I'll go down in my bare feet, just the same.'

'As you wish.' He collected her jacket, picked up her bag and shoes, and offered his arm. 'Will you at least accept a little friendly support on the way down?'

'Of course I will.' Her penitent eyes met his. 'I'm sorry I made you angry.'

'Hurt more than angry. You could kiss me better,' he added slyly.

She stood on tiptoe to aim for his cheek, but in her bare feet miscalculated the stretch and over-balanced against Joe so awkwardly he staggered, pulling her down with him as he fell on the sofa.

'Sorry,' Fen panted, her face hot with embarrass-ment as she struggled to lever herself up, but Joe chuckled and kept her sprawled on top of him. One arm held her still while his free hand brought her mouth down to his, and Fen melted against him. She raised her head after a while, and met a look in his eyes which set her body on fire.

'Sorry I squashed you,' she whispered.

'I'm neither sorry nor squashed,' he said, and shifted on his side, taking her with him to lie full length, face to face. 'What are you thinking?' he asked softly, his eyes looking deep into hers.

'I had this idea,' she said, trying to breathe nor-mally. 'You may not like it.'

'Try me.'

'I wondered whether you might like to teach me the difference—between sex and making love, I mean,' she added, in case he was in any doubt.

'You need to ask?' he said hoarsely, and kissed her deeply. Fen responded wildly, shivering as his hands traced spine-tingling paths over her bare shoulders. She felt his arousal hard against her as his mouth and tongue took possession of hers with the assurance that was so much part of him, waves of powerful feeling radiating from his body into every part of hers. 'You have a choice of location for night school,' he panted against her parted lips. 'Here. Or my bed.'

Fen's eyes glittered into his. 'We're both too tall for a sofa.'

'In that case—' Joe pulled her to her feet, then took her by the hand to lead her along the hall and up the steep stairs to the unknown territory of the second floor.

'Here be dragons,' she said breathlessly, as he took her into his bedroom.

'No. Just a mere ordinary, mortal male,' Joe said unevenly, and picked her up to lay her on his bed. He switched on lamps, drew the curtains across the windows, then came back to stand looking down at her. 'You're not heavy at all, but the stairs here are narrow, so I decided against carrying you all the way.'

She smiled. 'Probably just as well. In college I tripped and fell one day, and the bloke who tried to pick me up couldn't manage it.'

Joe sat on the bed beside her and took her hand. 'You were obviously a bit chubbier then.'

She shook her head. 'Not really. I've always been long and lanky.'

'Pure thoroughbred,' he said, kissing her long fingers.

Fen sat up, wreathing her arms round his neck. 'Listen, Joe. Because I wasn't straight with you about the dinner, I'd better make something clear. I badly need to feel wanted right now. But if you feel I'm making use of you, just to be held close like this, tell me now and I'll go right away, before—'

'Before what?' he said, against her mouth.

'Before I beg you to let me stay,' she said in a rush, and buried her head against his shoulder.

Joe crushed her close, then eased her down on the bed, holding her in an embrace with tenderness mingled with the hunger she could tell he was fighting to keep at bay as he kissed her.

'Is this the first lesson?' she whispered, drawing apart a little.

He nodded. 'First rule of the Tregenna course on making love. Comfort.'

'I'll remember,' she promised. 'What's the second?'

'Patience—which is the hard part for me.' He kissed her again with relish, tasting her as though she were some exotic fruit. His tongue outlined her lips, then slid between them to caress and inflame as he smoothed the straps of her top down over her shoulders, his entire body abruptly rigid when he found she was naked underneath.

Glorying in her effect on him, Fen trembled with excitement as Joe tossed the garment away. She sank her teeth into her bottom lip to keep from moaning when his clever fingers caressed her small, taut breasts, making magic that gradually became subtle torment. Her back arched, and she let out a choking gasp as his hands and lips and grazing teeth sent pure sensation searing through her body like lightning, from her nipples right down to her toes.

When Fen thought she might go up in smoke if Joe didn't stop, she uttered a choked cry of protest because he did. He slid up beside her and took her in his arms again, his cheek against hers.

'This isn't easy,' he panted, 'because I want you so much—which makes the patience part difficult.'

'Then let's get to the next part.' Her eyes luminous with invitation, she pulled away to slide off the far side of the bed. She stood erect to unpin her hair and shake it free, then in one sinuous movement she slithered out of her trousers and the scrap of black lace underneath. With a growl Joe launched himself across the bed to seize her and pull her back to him. He knelt over her while he ripped off his clothes, his eyes blazing with such heat Fen braced herself once he was naked, expecting him to take her there and then after such blatant provocation. But Joe held her face in his hands and smiled down into her eyes.

'Where were we?' he whispered.

'As far as I can remember,' she said with difficulty, 'we were still on the second lesson. The patience part.'

'You didn't help with that!'

Fen caught her breath, almost purring with pleasure while he traced kisses down her throat, then turned her over to brush her hair aside and kiss her from the nape of her neck down her spine, over the curves of her bottom and the backs of her thighs, his stroking, caressing hands following the route his mouth took on a journey which transformed her quivering, expectant body into one erogenous zone from head to foot. When he flipped her on her back at last she held up her arms and pulled him down to her, her hands moving feverishly over his shoulders as she kissed him with a wanton fervour designed to make it clear what she wanted next.

But Joe was possessed of patience Fen could only marvel at as he continued with his lesson. His skilled caresses brought her to such a peak of sensitivity she gasped and writhed against him, then gave a smothered, choked little sound when his fingers caused such hot, frantic turmoil inside her she dug her own into his back in entreaty.

And at last, when she thought she might go up

in flames if he didn't take her, Joe slid his hands beneath her hips, his kiss voracious as he thrust home into tight, wet heat, his groan almost of pain as her most secret muscles closed round him in ecstatic welcome. Brought to such an intense peak of arousal beforehand, the moment they were joined in panting, rhythmic union Fen found herself rushing towards a climax so overwhelming she cried out in hoarse astonishment against Joe's shoulder, just before he tensed, gasping, his body convulsed with the force of his own release.

'At least,' Fen muttered against Joe's shoulder minutes or hours later, when she'd recovered the power of speech, 'you don't need to ask how it was for me.'

'I could tell you enjoyed the lesson,' he said, laughter in his voice, and she grinned as she looked up at him.

'Revelled in it, you mean. You're a great teacher, Mr Tregenna.'

'With such a bright pupil it should have been easy, but it wasn't,' he said, and Fen shot upright, staring down at him in indignation.

'You mean it was hard work, making love to me?'

'Yes,' he said, and pulled her back down into his arms. 'When you did your striptease I wanted to throw myself on you and let nature take its course. Couldn't you tell?'

'For a minute I did think the lesson was likely to be short,' she admitted, deeply pleased. 'But in the end I was going crazy by the time you actually made love to me.' She felt her face grow hot. 'You must think I'm very easy to—to—'

'Bring to orgasm?' he said helpfully, then laughed uproariously when her eyes flashed green fire. 'Pax. Don't hit a man who can't retaliate.'

'Can't because I'm a female?' she demanded.

'No. Because at this moment I'm too weak to lift a finger.' He kissed her smiling mouth. 'For the time being, anyway. Stay here with me tonight, Fen,' he added, surprising her.

She moved away a little so she could see his face. 'Do you want that?'

'It would save me the trouble of driving you home,' he said, then grabbed her as she was about to leap from the bed. 'No, you don't. I was teasing. Of course I'll drive you to Farthing Street, if you insist. But that's Plan B.'

'What's Plan A?' she asked, mollified.

'I hold you in my arms all night, then make love to you again in the morning before I go off to earn my daily bread.'

Fen liked Plan A a lot, but she made a pretence of thinking it over as she looked round her at the big square room she hadn't paid much attention to earlier. 'You must earn enough for some butter on your bread—jam, too, if you can afford a place like this, Joe.'

'Crippling mortgage,' he explained sadly, then smiled. 'Stay with me, Fen.'

'On one condition.'

'Why do I feel apprehensive, I wonder?'

'I want to know what was in the parcel you brought round when you called for me tonight.'

'Automatic timers to fix to your light switches, so you don't get back to a dark house at night,' he said, his eyes narrowing at the sudden glitter of tears on her lashes. 'You'd have preferred chocolates?'

'*No!*' she said thickly, kicking his ankle with a bare toe. 'I'm just—well—touched.'

Joe stretched his long length against her, his mouth nuzzling her neck. 'After I went to the trouble of saving your life I might as well try to keep you in one piece.'

'You didn't save my life,' she said, trying to sound indignant. 'I did it myself. But I quite like having someone to watch out for me.'

'Good, because I think it only fair to point out that tonight's lesson was only the first in the course. You've got a way to go before you're ready to graduate.'

Fen smiled into his laughing eyes. 'Do you think I'm likely to pass?'

'You need a lot more lessons first,' he said earnestly.

'Do I?'

'Actually, no.' Joe grinned and hugged her close. 'But I do. I'm sold on this teaching idea. I've never done it before.'

'I don't want to hear about "before",' Fen said threateningly, then smiled at him, her eyes glowing. 'Thank you for showing me the difference, Joe. You must be a great teacher, because as well as making love it was cosmically terrific sex.'

CHAPTER SIX

FENELLA DYSART had never been in love before. She'd thought so more than once in the past, only to find she was mistaken when the parting of the ways came sooner rather than later. But with Joe Tregenna she was beginning to believe she'd found the real thing at last.

Their relationship had got off to a more rapid start than usual, she knew, due to the circumstances of their first encounter, because this had left Joe convinced she needed someone to watch over her. Though he flatly refused the title of guardian angel.

'There's nothing angelic about my feelings for you, Fenella Dysart,' he assured her.

'No,' she agreed, grinning. 'You're a devilish good teacher, Joe Tregenna. Do you think I'm a good pupil?'

'Brilliant.'

'So do you think I'll pass?'

'You already have!'

When Fen was alone during the day, with time to think, she felt utterly devastated because Adam had made no further effort to contact her. But when she was with Joe the sheer pleasure of his company made up for everything else that was wrong in her life.

Dining out had lost its attraction after the disastrous evening at the Mitre, and Fen preferred to stay at home in Chester Square with Joe, or even in her bedroom in Farthing Street. And when the weather allowed they spent hours in the garden behind his flat, happy just to sit and talk. They found they enjoyed the same kind of food, shared a similar sense of humour, agreed on some subjects and disagreed amicably about others. And their lovemaking was everything she'd never even dreamed of before.

But, although Joe kept nagging her to leave the house in Farthing Street, he never suggested she move into Chester Square with him. It was almost, she thought, on one of her runs along the river, as though they needed to reach some other stage in their relationship before he committed himself. Maybe he'd had his fingers too recently burned by Melissa. Or maybe he was waiting to see if Safehouse offered Fenella Dysart a job. The possibility that he had no intention of asking her to live with him was something she refused to contemplate.

The moment the Safehouse advertisement was in the paper, Fen sent off for an application form, filled it in and posted it, and received a letter by return asking her to present herself for interview the following Monday.

'You'll be fine,' said Joe, while Fen helped him unpack the endless boxes the removal company had delivered. 'But don't wear the black dress. The head of Human Resources is the conventional type. He won't go for bare legs and cleavage.'

'Legs I've got, but I plead not very guilty in the cleavage department,' she said regretfully.

He gave her a blood-heating look as he wrenched open a box. 'I lust after you just the way you are. Dirty face included.'

'No point in washing until we've finished this lot,' she said, deliberately cheerful to hide a familiar pang. It was exciting and deeply gratifying to be desired so fiercely. But she wanted Joe to love her as well. He *made* love to her with all the skill and passion she could ever want, but Fen was already so fathoms deep in love with him she yearned to hear him utter the three magic little words she had to fight to keep back every time she was in his arms.

'No point in giving in to the urge to take you to bed right now, either,' he agreed, with deep regret.

'It's not even midday yet,' she said primly.

'I fail to see what that has to do with anything.' Joe took a pile of books from her and dumped them on the floor, then took her in his arms and kissed her. 'It's good to be able to kiss a girl without stooping,' he told her, rubbing noses.

'I take it Melissa was petite?' said Fen, resigned.

'Small, but vicious,' he agreed, and shook his head. 'Why do I attract women with such tempers, I wonder?'

'Your sunny disposition, I suppose—attraction of opposites.' She pushed him away. 'Now, tell me where you want this lot and let's get on.'

Joe ordered dinner in from a local Thai restaurant later, and afterwards they settled down together on one of the sofas to watch a film on television while Fen tried to bring herself to mention something she'd been trying to tell Joe all day.

'You know, I rather liked the fringe benefits of watching television in your bedroom,' he said regretfully.

Fen giggled. 'I've never heard it referred to as fringe benefits before. And this way,' she pointed out severely, 'at least we get to see the end of the film.'

'True. What shall we do tomorrow? I vote we drive out to lunch somewhere—'

'Actually,' she said, swinging her legs to the

floor, 'I can't tomorrow. I'm having lunch with a friend.'

Joe sat up in surprise, pushing his hair back. 'You said you didn't have any here.'

'My best friend Laura's home for the weekend.'

'Why didn't you mention it before? I assumed you'd spend the entire weekend with me.' His eyes narrowed. 'Or was I ruffling your feathers by taking too much for granted again?'

'No. In fact,' she added deliberately, 'I'd be very happy to call here afterwards, if you want. Or maybe you could come to Farthing Street later on?'

Joe's face relaxed slightly. 'What time will you be back?'

'If you come round about six I'll make supper.' She got to her feet. 'Time I was off.'

'*What?*' He stared at her blankly. 'Why? I thought we were going to bed.'

'I can't stay tonight, because I've got to be up early,' she said firmly, having planned this in advance as part of her campaign to make Joe see how much better it would be to have her living with him than the present arrangement.

'Surely you can drive back first thing in the morning, Fen?'

'I'd rather go now.'

His eyes hardened. 'In other words you don't want to sleep with me tonight.'

Fen looked at him squarely. 'Joe, we spent an outrageously long siesta in your bed this afternoon, instead of unpacking the rest of your gear.'

He got slowly to his feet, looking down his nose at her. 'You're rationing your favours now?'

'Favours?' She held on to her temper with difficulty. Careful, she warned herself. Be cool. 'And there was I, thinking we were making love. Obviously I haven't got it quite right yet.'

'Then come to bed and I'll give you another lesson,' he said triumphantly, and held out his hand, smiling, so supremely confident of victory she shook her head.

If he'd looked less confident Fen would have been tempted. But if she gave in now Joe might well assume he had only to snap his fingers in future for her to agree to anything he wanted. 'Perhaps we can postpone that,' she suggested.

Which wiped his smile away. And in sudden foreboding Fen realised that for the first time in their acquaintance Joe Tregenna was about to lose his temper.

'It's pointless for you to go back to that bloody awful house tonight,' he said angrily. 'Stay here.'

Confronted with an order, Fen shook her head. 'Not tonight,' she said coolly, and collected her bag and jacket.

Surely he wasn't going to let her go like that? All she had to do to close the sudden chasm yawning between them was to walk a couple of steps and hold up her face to be kissed. But then he'd assume she'd capitulated. And some ingrained spirit of independence baulked at that. She stared into his eyes, which were cold and implacable beneath half-closed lids. When he remained obdurately silent she turned away, and, forcing herself to walk slowly, she went to the door and closed it quietly behind her before racing downstairs to her car.

Her cellphone was mute on the way back to Farthing Street, but once inside Fen was so sure that Joe was just giving her time to get back she ran to her bedroom to be ready when he rang. But when she put it back on charge the phone remained silent, and she spent a sleepless night of misery, convinced she'd made a terrible mistake.

She delayed as long as possible before leaving the house next morning, but there was no phone call. Fen set off on her drive with a heavy heart. Several times during the journey she almost gave in and rang Joe's number, but each time she drew back. He might be hostile. And right now hostility was the last thing she needed.

With twenty miles or so to drive, tense with apprehension about her welcome when she arrived, Fen felt weary when she finally reached the winding drive that led up through tiered gardens to Friars Wood, home to several generations of Dysarts. Her heart beating thickly, she did a U-turn and parked in front of the converted stable block, with the car facing in the right direction for the hurried departure which in worst-case scenario might be necessary. She walked slowly to the main house, feet dragging and eyes wistful as she looked down past the summerhouse over the garden towards the little wood, where wild anemones and bluebells grew in season. Squaring her shoulders, she walked up the steps to the front door, and rang the bell.

Fen heard loud, familiar barking, but no one came to the door. She waited for a while, then rang again, but with the same result. She peered through the glazed upper half of the door, but the house looked deserted. Fen tossed her keys hand to hand for a moment, then took in a deep breath and unlocked the door.

'Adam?' she called. 'Gabriel?'

But other than the frantic barking in the scullery there was no answer. The study was empty, there was no smell of Sunday roast in the kitchen, and not a soul to greet her except Pan, the retriever, who flattened himself on the tiled floor of the scullery in an ecstasy of welcome when she dropped on her knees to hug him and stroke his gleaming gold coat.

'Where is everyone, Pan?' she asked, laughing

unsteadily as he licked her face. His tail wagging furiously, the dog kept close while Fen went on a tour of the other rooms, and waited obediently at the foot of the stairs while she went to check the bedrooms. But she knew she wouldn't find anyone. Adam had taken his family out, probably for the day.

Numb with disappointment, Fen gave in to the frisking dog's entreaties, collected his lead from a hook in the scullery and took him for a walk through the gardens. 'I'm not letting you run, Pan,' she told the panting dog, 'because if you took off and got lost, like your dad did once, Adam would go ballistic. And I'm in enough trouble with him already.'

She did a prolonged tour of the gardens, crunched her way through the undergrowth in the wood for Pan to sniff and investigate to his heart's content, then went back to the house with him and refilled his water bowl. After a tearful, lengthy farewell, she shut him in the scullery, locked the front door, and trudged back to the Stables. At one time Adam's bachelor home, the Stables would shortly house his parents, and the vivid, primary colours he'd chosen for himself were being replaced by the more subtle shades preferred by his mother. Fen took a peep in at the windows, then with a last look at the main house got in the car and drove down the steep bends of the drive and on down the lane past the farm, to the main road which would take her back to Pennington.

Fen drove slowly, through pouring rain which sluiced down the windscreen like tears. When she arrived in Farthing Street, too weary and heartsore even to make coffee, she went straight upstairs to lie on the bed with only the silent cellphone for company. Staring dry-eyed at the ceiling, she lay still and drained after the fruitless journey, so motionless and full of multiple-choice misery that eventually nature took over. She fell into a sleep so deep she felt as though she were coming back from another planet when she stirred at last to the sound of hammering on the front door below her bedroom window. Pushing her hair from her eyes, she slid out of bed to peer out, and with a leap of joy saw Joe's car parked at the kerb.

The hammering resumed on the back door, and Fen raced downstairs on bare feet to open it. Wild-eyed and pale beneath his tan, Joe came in like a hurricane, slamming the door behind him.

'Why the hell didn't you answer when I knocked?' he demanded, out of breath.

She blinked owlishly, securing her hair behind her ears as she backed away. 'I was asleep.'

'All this time? I've been knocking for God knows how long.'

'I was out for the count.'

'Alone?'

'You mean love in the afternoon?' she snapped. 'No. Why are you here?'

Joe closed his eyes for an instant, then opened them on hers. 'It's after six. You invited me to supper.'

'Is it that late?' she said, giddy with relief because he was actually here, after all. 'I've slept for hours.'

'Lucky you.' His jaw tightened. 'I haven't.'

'Why?'

'Because we had a fight, if you remember.'

'Of course I remember.'

They looked at each other in a silence which grew to such proportions in the ugly little room that Fen was ready to scream by the time Joe spoke.

'Did you enjoy lunch with your friend?' he said politely.

'I didn't have any lunch. There was no one at home. I must have mistaken the date.' Fen eyed Joe's taut face in indecision. 'If you'll sit down I'll make supper,' she offered at last, half expecting him to refuse.

After an agonising moment, when it seemed likely he would, Joe nodded. 'Can I help?'

If he'd take her in his arms and kiss her senseless it would help a lot, but that, Fen could see, wasn't going to happen any time soon. Hoping a spot of domesticity might soften him up, she suggested he lay the table. 'You know where everything is. I can't offer you the Sunday papers; I didn't get any today.'

He shrugged. 'I've read them from cover to cover already.'

'Listen to the radio, then. I won't be long.'

The linen trousers and shirt Fen had chosen so carefully for her visit to Friars Wood were in a bad way after her nap. And Joe looked good, as usual, in well-worn jeans and a thin blue shirt. Afraid he might take off if she took time to change into something similar, Fen ground her teeth in sudden exasperation at the way she'd changed lately from the totally confident creature she had been all her life into someone expecting the worst all the time. She stared moodily at her reflection as she brushed her hair. Joe could take her the way she was, crumpled and creased, with only a touch of lipstick as a gesture to grooming.

'What else can I do?' he asked, when she rejoined him at the kitchen table, which looked a good deal better hidden by a blue and white checked cloth and set with the plates and silverware Fen had bought herself.

'You could cut some bread, then just sit down and talk to me while I heat up the sauce and put the pasta to boil,' she said, and got busy.

Joe took her at her word, keeping to the impersonal by discussing some of the articles he'd read in the paper while he watched every move she made as she emptied prepared salad leaves from a packet, tossed them with oil and lemon juice, then drained the pasta and added the sauce she'd made herself the day before.

Fen stared uneasily at her steaming bowl when she sat down, afraid that the first mouthful would choke her.

Joe put out a hand and touched hers. 'You must be hungry, Fen. Come on—dig in so I can do the same.'

Which was all it took for her appetite to revive, and Fen began to eat with the enjoyment she brought to most of her meals. Taught to cook early in life, she felt a warm rush of pleasure when Joe complimented her on the sauce.

'Best I've tasted,' he assured her, then grinned. 'What brand is it?'

'Dysart secret recipe.'

A few minutes later every leaf of salad and hunk of bread had been wolfed down, and their pasta bowls wiped clean.

'Wonderful,' said Joe, and smiled ruefully. 'I didn't have lunch either.'

'Why not?'

'You know exactly why!'

Much cheered by this, Fen washed up while Joe made coffee, then sat down at the table to drink

it, flushing a little when she met the wry gleam
in his eyes.

'I'm not rationing my favours, as you put it so
beautifully, Joe,' she assured him tartly. 'But I'm
not suggesting a move up to my bedroom either,
because it's time we had a talk. There are things
I need to tell you face to face.'

'And in the unlikely event that I'm invited to get
comfortable on your bed, you think I won't pay
attention.'

'Exactly.' Fen drank down some of her coffee
and took in a deep breath. 'Look, Joe, I lied about
having lunch with Laura. As far as I know she's
in London, probably spending the day with the
current man in her life.'

Joe frowned. 'You mean you stayed here all
day?'

'No.' She flicked at her crumpled shirt with distaste. 'This is my version of sackcloth and ashes.
I went to see Adam.'

'Did you, indeed? To kiss and make up?'

'Not exactly. I needed a favour.'

Fen described how she'd steeled herself to drive
over to Stavely, to see Adam and Gabriel and their
children, hoping to get an invitation to lunch.

'Was that likely, in the circumstances?' said Joe
curiously.

'Probably not. But I wanted to see Adam before
tomorrow because on my application form to

Safehouse Insurance I gave his name as my referee.' Fen shrugged at the look on Joe's face. 'I had no alternative. I could have put Tim Mathias, but a couple of weeks behind the bar at the Mitre didn't seem much of a recommendation, whereas I worked for Adam for over a year before the quarrel. And in my vacations well before that.'

'So your job here in Pennington was at the family auction house,' said Joe, enlightened. 'What did you do?'

'I worked as Adam's assistant when the lady who'd been there for ever finally retired. Adam took a lot of persuading that I was up to the job, but I was confident I could cope because I'd worked with Mrs Bates in vacations for years before she retired. I'm computer literate, good at figures, and I've been familiar with the antiques trade all my life. Adam needn't have worried. I was a great success at it,' added Fen without conceit.

'So why did you leave?'

'We had the quarrel.'

'What was it about?' Joe waited, watching her gnaw her lip. 'Or would you be revealing family secrets to tell me?'

'I'm sorry, but I would.' She gave him a direct look. 'Is it an obstacle? To our being friends, I mean?'

'No. Though I think of our relationship in much warmer terms than that.' Joe reached across and took her hand. 'Last night, after you'd gone, I did some hard thinking. My bed was cold and lonely without you, darling.'

Fen gazed at him, heart thumping. 'You could have rung to tell me that.'

'I would have, but by the time I finally got to sleep for a couple of hours I didn't wake until midday, and, just like you, I needed to see you face to face to have my say.'

'I wish I'd known that,' she said frankly. 'I drove back from Stavely feeling like death.'

'A thought which occurred to me when you didn't answer the door,' said Joe grimly. 'Because your car was here I began imagining all kinds of things which frightened the hell out of me.'

'I could have been out for a run.'

'I know. I told myself that. But I didn't believe it.' He shrugged. 'It brought something home to me.'

'What?'

'If you shared my flat I wouldn't have to worry about you any more.' His eyes locked with hers and he reached out the other hand so that both hers were grasped tightly in his. 'What do you say?'

If he'd made the suggestion the day before a rapturous, instant yes would have been his answer, thought Fen sadly. But a whole sleepless night spent in ruthless self-analysis had put a very different spin on her life. 'Joe, I would love to share your gorgeous flat with you. But not yet. Before that I need to do some serious spring cleaning in my life. If you still want me after I've done it I'll be happy—deliriously happy—to live with you.'

Joe got up, pulling her with him, and took her in his arms, rubbing his cheek against hers. 'Not exactly the answer I hoped for, but a whole lot better than the no I fully expected after your exit last night.'

'I hoped you'd come after me and sweep me up in your arms and take me to bed,' she said frankly, and grinned at him. 'When you didn't a dignified exit was my only option.'

Joe's eyes lit with an explicit gleam. 'If I tried the sweeping up bit right now, what would happen?'

'You might run out of steam by the time we get to my room,' she teased, then smiled at him luminously. 'So, because I'm in crying need of some cuddling, I'd be very happy if you'd just follow me upstairs, Mr Tregenna.'

'So would I,' he said with feeling.

When they reached her bedroom Fen drew the curtains on the summer gloom and Joe came behind her and locked his arms round her waist, his mouth in the hollow of her ear.

'It's twenty-nine hours and twelve minutes since I made love to you,' he informed her, and drew her down on the bed, kneeling over her as he began to undo her shirt. 'So be warned. I intend to relish every little step of the way.'

'And where are all—these—steps—leading?' she gasped, as his mouth and hands moved over the places he was exposing, making love to her body with expert, tormenting caresses that filled her with joy even while they drove her crazy.

'Heaven,' he whispered at last, and slid over her and into her, his mouth and body taking possession of hers as they came together with total abandon, their senses heightened to fever pitch by their rift.

Fen lay limp and motionless while the throbbing aftermath of climax died away, and Joe raised his head at last, his hand gentle as he brushed the tumbled hair away from her face. 'Are you still with me?'

'I will be, eventually.' She smiled up at him. 'If I do come to live with you—'

'When, not if,' he corrected.

'When I come to live with you it won't always be desperate and frantic like that, will it?'

'No.' He sighed theatrically. 'Sometimes I'll be too tired, or you'll have a headache.'

'It's not my style to make excuses, Joe,' she said tartly. 'If I don't want to make love I'll just say no. And you must do the same.'

He raked a hand through sweat-dampened hair,

his lips twitching. 'I can't see myself saying no to you, somehow.'

'You might.'

'And pigs might fly.' Joe rubbed his cheek against hers. 'I suppose I should go home tonight. You need some sleep before your interview.'

Fen shot upright and pulled the quilt up to her chin, her eyes suddenly wide with apprehension. 'Which may be a waste of time. What happens if Adam refuses a reference?'

He frowned as he stood up to dress. 'He wouldn't go as far as that, surely?'

'I don't think so. I just wish they'd been at home today.' Her mouth drooped. 'It wasn't easy for me to drive to Stavely today, Joe.'

'I'll bet it wasn't.'

'I should have gone to see Adam at Dysart's on Friday, or even yesterday morning. Bearded the lion in his den. But I thought it better to talk to him on home ground today instead.' She blinked back tears. 'And, to be honest, I was longing to see Gabriel and the boys. I miss them terribly. But at least I saw the dog. Pan gave me such a huge welcome I took him for a walk before I left.'

Joe pulled her into his arms and held her close. 'The sooner you sort things out with Adam the better, Fen. Which is not an entirely disinterested observation, because then I can have you out of this dump and safe with me in Chester Square.'

Fen clung to him, hating to see him go, especially when he told her he would be away for a few days in the head office in London.

'And when I come back we must talk. I have something to tell you,' he said, as he left.

'Tell me now!'

'When I come back,' he insisted, and kissed her. 'Something for you to think about while I'm away.'

Fen thought about it a lot, and presented herself for interview at Safehouse Insurance the following afternoon wishing she could see Joe's encouraging face as she entered the bright, modern building. But it would be Thursday before she saw him again. It was a depressing thought she put from her mind as she gave her name to the receptionist, who rang the head of Human Resources to announce her arrival.

David Baker was a pleasant man in his forties, who surprised Fen by coming to collect her. He conducted her up stairs curving from the foyer to a bright, open-plan call centre, where employees of both sexes were hard at work in front of computers installed in groups along desktops that snaked through the light, airy room in serpentine fashion—very different from the conventional rows of desks Fen had visualised.

She was taken into an office with a view of

Pennington rooftops, and faced David Baker across his desk as he went through her application. The interview was brief, but very thorough, with the expected sticky moment when it came to her reason for leaving the family business.

'I felt it was time to branch out on my own, to be independent,' she explained, which sounded horribly lame to her own ears.

David Baker gave no indication of his own opinion, and after a few more questions gave her some information about salary and conditions, then took her back downstairs and told her she would be hearing from him in a day or so.

New to the process of job interviews, Fen felt frustrated. She had wanted a yes or no straight away. She hoped Joe had put in the good word he'd promised, and drove back to Farthing Street, wondering how to pass the time until he came back. Tonight, she decided, she would see a double bill at the Regal cinema, and tomorrow she would go for a long run, rent a video, and buy all the books she could afford.

It amazed her to think that until a short time ago she hadn't known Joe Tregenna existed. But she did now. And couldn't imagine life without him.

CHAPTER SEVEN

THE days dragged, as expected, while Joe was away. But after his nightly phone calls Fen went to sleep happy after hearing how much he missed her. And Joe never failed to issue strict instructions on security now he wasn't around to take care of her himself.

'I keep telling you, Joe. I can take care of myself.'

'I'd rather do it for you,' he said, in a tone which made her pulse race. 'So be good until I get back.'

'And after that?'

'I'll tell you when I see you,' he promised.

Fen had received no reply from Safehouse Insurance by the day Joe was due back. Afraid this meant they were going to turn her down, she felt edgy and restless, certain by now that Adam had refused to give her a reference. She sat staring into space at the kitchen table, more convinced by the minute that she was right. Adam had made

Tim sack her from the Mitre, so maybe he'd also sabotaged her chances of a job with Safehouse.

Her gut reaction was to rush round to Dysart's and confront Adam in his office. But common sense warned that he might not be alone. And, however much anger and hurt she felt towards Adam, she had no desire to broadcast their differences to the staff, some of whom had been with Dysart's for years. She made herself wait for a while to achieve calm, then rang the auction house.

'Mr Dysart's office,' said an unfamiliar female voice.

'Could I speak to Mr Dysart, please?' said Fen, taken aback.

'I'm sorry, he's not due back until later. Can I take a message?'

'Would you please tell him that Fenella Dysart would like to see him? Perhaps he'd give me an appointment,' she added, with sarcasm wasted on the woman at the other end.

'Certainly. If you'll give me your number I'll arrange a time and ring you back after I've spoken to him.'

Had Adam replaced her already? Enraged, Fen wanted to storm up and down like an angry tigress. Because that was physically impossible in Farthing Street she drove to her favourite spot by the river and went for a very long run instead. She bought some food on the way back, in case Joe arrived in time for supper, then channelled her still seething energies into cleaning the ugly little house from top to bottom.

Tired out at last, Fen took a bath later in the newly scoured tub, then spent a long time fiddling with her hair before dressing in skin-tight white jeans and a clinging scarlet top. Afterwards, left without another thing to do, she sat at the table with a cup of coffee, trying to get interested in a book while she waited for the minutes to crawl by until Joe came.

When she heard footsteps pass by the window at last Fen's heart leapt. She threw the book down and ran to open the door. But her radiant smile of welcome died abruptly at the sight of Adam Dysart.

'You wanted to see me, Fenny?' He smiled wryly. 'I thought I'd have more luck if I came to your back door this time.'

'You'd better come in.' She turned on her heel, leaving him to follow. Adam, tall and magnificent in one of his formal suits, stopped dead on the threshold, his eyes wide with disbelief as he looked round the kitchen.

'In God's name, why, Fenny?' he demanded.

'I might ask the same of you,' she said coldly.

'What do you mean?'

'Oh, come *on*. Don't play the innocent.' She

thrust a hand through her hair, destroying the effect she'd taken so long to achieve. 'Did it give you enormous satisfaction to refuse a reference?'

He frowned. 'But I didn't, Fenny. If you mean the insurance job—though why the hell you want it beats me—I gave them a positively glowing reference. Gabriel said it was the least I could do after getting you sacked from the Mitre.'

She stared at him, deflated, knowing Adam well enough to accept this as the truth.

'I sent it off to these Safehouse people by return of post.' He leaned against the doorjamb, looking at her with something she recognised with a wrench as compassion. 'Not heard from them yet, Fenny?'

'No,' she admitted, mortified.

'You will. They're bound to want you. Though if you're determined to turn your back on Dysart's there must be more exciting jobs out there.'

'I didn't even aspire to exciting,' she retorted. 'I just needed any job I could get after you had me thrown out of the Mitre.'

'I did that for a purpose,' he said, with a lack of repentance that touched Fen on the raw.

'What harm was I doing?' she flung at him.

'None. Though why you should prefer working there instead of at Dysart's I fail to see. With Tim in command I could just about swallow the bar work, but when I saw you perched on that piano I saw red.' Adam threw out a hand. 'And in my insensitive, typical male fashion—I'm quoting Gabriel here—I assumed that if you had no job you'd come back to work with me at Dysart's. Preferably before Mother and Dad get home from their cruise and find out what you've been up to.' He sighed wearily. 'When the insurance people asked for a reference I realised I was wrong.'

'You actually thought that getting me sacked would bring me running back to you?' said Fenny in disbelief.

Adam smiled wryly. 'All right, I admit I went about it the wrong way, so don't lose that famous temper of yours.'

'Which reminds me,' she said ominously. 'Why did you ignore me at the Mitre that night? Couldn't you bring yourself to acknowledge me once I'd fled the nest?'

'I was still angry with you at that point,' he admitted, and rubbed a hand through his curling black hair. 'But for God's sake, Fenny, let's stop all this now. Gabriel's in a terrible state.'

Fen bit her lip. 'I feel bad about that. Tell Gabriel I'm sorry I upset *her*, at least,' she added pointedly. 'Go away and do it right now, in fact. I'm expecting someone.'

Adam stood like a rock, arms folded. 'You asked me to come, so I'm not leaving until we sort things out.' He gave her a mocking smile. 'I take it your new friend is about to appear?'

'Actually, he's my lover!'

He laughed. 'Was that meant to shock me, Fen? You took pains to ram that down my throat the night you slammed your door in my face.'

She shrugged. 'We weren't then. But we are now.'

'Who is he? What does he do?'

'Not that it's any business of yours, but his name's Joe Tregenna, and, unlike you and your glamorous, ready-made job, he sells insurance.'

'Good for him,' said Adam, unmoved. 'But tell me, Fenny, does he know that you went running from the job ready-made for *you*? And, worse than that, left Gabriel and me in a hell of a state when we found you'd taken all your things and cleared off while we were out. And instead of a note left your phone on your bed,' he added grimly, 'so we couldn't contact you.'

Her chin lifted. 'I just had to get away after Gabriel let the cat out of the bag.'

The dark eyes turned flint-hard. 'None of this is Gabriel's fault.'

'I know, I know!'

'Then it's time you convinced her of that, because she feels as though it is. You've caused my wife a lot of grief, Fenella Dysart.'

Her eyes fell. 'I'm sorry about that. Truly. Tell

Gabriel that I'm not blaming her in the slightest.' Her head went up. 'But I am blaming you, Adam, and everyone else in the family, for keeping me in the dark all my life. Can you imagine how it felt to have my identity suddenly stripped from me?'

'Perhaps,' said Adam grimly, 'it was something similar to our feelings when you went missing. And it took your friend Laura, not you, to ring from London to say you were safe.'

'It was nothing to do with Laura,' said Fen militantly. 'She had no right to interfere. We had such a blazing row about it I couldn't stay in her flat, as planned. At which point it dawned on me that I could get back at you much better by working in a pub right here in Pennington than in London.' She looked him in the eye. 'I knew you'd hate the idea of a Dysart working behind a bar right here under your nose, so I got the job at the Mitre to annoy you.'

'Until Tim Mathias rang me to say you'd asked for a job I thought you were staying with Laura in London to cool off for a bit. Instead you prefer to live in a slum, instead of your own home at Friars Wood, and work behind a bar. And all because I said you were a spoilt brat who needed to grow up and consider other people's feelings,' said Adam scathingly. 'Thank God Mother and Dad weren't around.'

Fen winced. 'But that's the point,' she said

fiercely. 'They're not my parents, are they? Until a month ago I believed I was their daughter, and your sister. Then by pure chance I discover that I'm just someone's by-blow, a little bas—'

'Don't you dare!' growled Adam.

'I should have been told,' she said stubbornly.

'I agree. We all did.' He looked suddenly tired. 'But it was Mother and Dad's job to do that, and they kept putting it off until the time was right. Then the time arrived when they weren't there to pick up the pieces. But you're no one's *by-blow*,' he added forcibly.

'I feel like one. You told me my mother was Rachel Dysart, but who exactly is my father? Did she even know?' Fen threw at him. 'She was getting on by the time she had me, so did she just pop into a sperm bank when her clock ticked too loudly? Or am I the result of sun and sex on a holiday fling?'

'That's enough,' Adam roared, glaring at her in outrage. 'Don't talk about Rachel like that.'

'Sorry,' muttered Fen, suddenly ashamed. She hesitated, then looked at him in appeal. 'I've seen photographs, but what was she really like?'

Adam's eyes softened a little. 'For a start she was Dad's only sister—and my aunt—long before she was your mother. I was very fond of her. We all were. She was good-looking, highly intelligent, and a committed career woman with no interest in commitment, apparently, until she met your father. They fell in love, but had to keep it secret from everyone because he was married.'

'You mean they had an affair,' said Fen in disgust. 'And of course he didn't want to be saddled with a little embarrassment when—when Rachel died after giving birth to me.'

Adam looked at her with compassion. 'He never knew about you, Fenny. He was killed in a road accident months before you were born. Rachel was so heartbroken she didn't look after herself properly, contracted pneumonia, and eventually gave birth to you prematurely. Mother and Dad hadn't even known she was pregnant. They rushed to London to the hospital, utterly devastated to find Rachel so ill.' His mouth compressed. 'She lived just long enough for them to promise her you would be brought up in their loving care. Which you have been.'

Secretly deeply moved, Fen swallowed hard. 'But I still should have been told! Everybody on the planet knew except me,' she said huskily, tears welling in her eyes. She knuckled them away, then shrugged defiantly. 'At least it's no big thing to be illegitimate these days, if it's still called that.'

'It doesn't apply to you, anyway. Mother and Dad adopted you legally.' He smiled at her. 'You've always been ours, Fenny, right from the beginning.'

She was quiet for a moment, taking this in, then shot Adam an apprehensive look. 'You still haven't told me who my father was.'

Adam hesitated, then took her by the shoulders. 'To save you unnecessary nightmares, Fenny, he was Richard Savage.'

She stiffened, staring up at him in horror. 'But— but how could he *do* that to a wife like Helen? She's disabled!'

'Think about it.' Adam increased his grip as she tried to break away. 'Perhaps now you've got a lover, as you're so keen to tell me, you can try to understand. In her twenties Helen suffered a brain haemorrhage which put paid to the physical side of her marriage, and though Richard was devoted to her, and took every care of her, the inevitable happened when he fell in love with Rachel. But they kept their secret so well Helen knew nothing about it until you were nearly seven years old.'

Fen bit down on a trembling lower lip. 'But she's always so loving towards me.'

'Love at first sight,' agreed Adam. 'Just like the rest of us. You've always been spoilt rotten by everyone in the family. Which is *your* family, too, and always has been. Remember this, Fenella Dysart. You're my sister legally, and in every other way, and, drama queen though you are, I love you,' said Adam. He gave her a little shake, then released her to glance at his watch. 'I must go. My turn to get the boys to bed. So,' he added, as he went to the door, 'are you coming back to Dysart's, Fenny?'

'Do you still want me?' she said thickly, and blew her nose.

He smiled. 'Of course I still want you.'

'Who was the woman I spoke to on the phone?'

'The temp I took on until you deign to favour Dysart's with your services again.'

'In that case I'd better get back to my office and sort it out before the parents get back—' Her mouth twisted. 'Or should I be calling them Frances and Tom now?'

'If you want to break their hearts, yes,' Adam snapped, and moved back to tap her cheek with a warning finger. 'Try to get in a better frame of mind by then, little sister. In the meantime I'll give the temporary Mrs Price her notice, and expect you next Monday morning on the dot, unless I see you sooner. Which I would prefer,' he added, kissing her cheek, 'so for God's sake come home.'

'Thank you,' said Fen shakily. 'How are the boys?'

'They keep asking for you.'

'I came to see you last Sunday,' she blurted, 'but you weren't there.'

Adam stared at her aghast. 'Oh, Fen, what hellish timing! We were with Gabriel's parents. Don't cry, sweetheart. Come here.' He swept her into his familiar embrace, hugging her close. 'Time to come home, Fenny. We all miss you.'

'Soon,' she promised, reluctant to spoil the moment by telling him her plans to move in with Joe. 'Give my love to Gabriel, and kiss the boys for me.'

He ruffled her hair, smiling at her like the old Adam who'd been there for her all her life. 'Now I must go,' he said, and went to the door, shaking his head as he looked round the kitchen. 'This is one terrible dump, Fenny.'

'Chosen with enormous care, partly as hair shirt and partly to make you sorry you'd been so horrible to me,' she said, smiling through her wet lashes. 'Thank you for coming, Adam.'

'I would have done long before this, but Gabriel persuaded me you needed time to adjust.' He tapped his watch. 'Your time just ran out.'

After Adam had gone Fen sat slumped at the table for a while, feeling as if a great burden had rolled from her shoulders, then her eyes lit up as she heard the familiar tattoo on the door. She flew to open it and Joe, in a formal suit, gave her a smile which decided her against flinging herself into his arms.

'Hi,' she said, crestfallen, as he walked past her into the room. 'You just missed Adam.'

'I know. I saw him leave.' He watched as she

bolted the door. 'I see you're keeping up with security.'

She gazed at him blankly. Polite conversation after an absence of four days?

'A pity you hadn't closed the window properly instead,' he went on casually, 'particularly while Adam was here.'

Fen stiffened. 'Why?'

Joe gave her a smile which froze her blood. 'I meant to come in and announce myself, but when I heard an argument I did some eavesdropping. And soon wished I hadn't.'

She stared at him in growing dismay. 'I wish you hadn't, too,' she said, after a taut silence. 'I wanted to tell you my pathetic little story myself.'

Joe perched on a corner of the table, his eyes harder than she'd ever imagined they could be. 'Ah, but would it have been the same story?'

Fen sat down abruptly. 'What do you mean?'

'Human nature what it is,' he said, as if he were discussing some abstract problem, 'you would have given me a carefully edited version, presumably omitting the insults you flung at your birth mother, plus the fact that you drove Adam and his wife demented by running away.' His mouth twisted in distaste. 'I agree with Adam. Spoilt brat just about sums it up.'

Fen sat looking at him dumbly. At last, feeling

unutterably weary, she got to her feet. 'If that's how you feel you can go.'

'I will. But I need to know something first.' Joe stood up, his eyes searching. 'Do you feel *any* regret for the worry you caused, or even the things you said?'

'Yes, I do,' she said coldly. 'I told Adam you were my lover. I regret saying that, because it isn't true, is it?'

'It was until I got here tonight. Then I discovered that the Fenella Dysart I thought I knew doesn't actually exist.' His eyes stabbed hers. 'You've been stringing me along like a con-artist, playing on my sympathy with your tall tales about being an orphan. And Adam Dysart, far from being the cruel cousin, is a brother who loves you enough to forgive you everything. Why the hell did you lie to me?' he added roughly.

'I didn't actually lie! I just left things out. Personal, family things, the kind one doesn't tell a stranger.'

'Stranger or not, I want to hear. Are there more Dysarts?'

'Three sisters, as well as Adam. Leonie is married to Jonah Savage—' Fen halted. 'How much did your eavesdropping tell you?' she asked dully. 'Did you get to the part where Adam told me about my father?'

'Yes. Though obviously the name meant nothing to me.'

'It's a bit complicated. My sister Leo is married to Jonah Savage, the nephew of Richard Savage, who, although he was married, fell in love with my mother and fathered me,' she said, as though reading from a cue-card. 'Which makes Jonah my cousin as well as my brother-in-law. Weird!'

'Any more revelations?'

'Why should you be interested—now?'

'Why not?' Again the unsettling smile. 'In the circumstances I feel entitled to know both sides of the story.'

'There are no sides,' she said without expression. 'And it's not a story. It's my life. But, if you want the entire *dramatis personae*, my parents are Tom and Frances Dysart. Leonie is their eldest, married to Jonah. Jess is married to Lorenzo Forli and lives in Florence. You know Adam's married to Gabriel, and lastly there's Kate, the brilliant one, who works in pharmaceutical research with her husband Alasdair Drummond and is expecting their first child. The others have eight children between them, so far. And that's it,' Fen ended wearily. 'The Dysart Dynasty complete.'

'Not quite,' Joe reminded her. 'You left your name off the list.'

'So I did. Fenella is the youngest, and Dysart twice over, it seems—both by birth and adoption.'

She gave him a mirthless little smile. 'My childhood was as idyllic as yours. And in my teens I never took to recreational substances, excess alcohol, body-piercing and so on. I never felt the least need to rebel, the way my friends did. My family even looked on my steady stream of boyfriends as safety in numbers. Then a few weeks ago Gabriel innocently let slip something about my birth which sent me raging to confront Adam. You know the rest.

'Afterwards I pleaded time alone to recover, instead of going out to lunch with the others. While they were out of the way I packed my bags and instead of a note left my phone on my bed, which meant they couldn't contact me. I took off to London to stay with my friend Laura, but she was the first one Adam rang and had already told him I was on my way. Blazing row number two. So I went back to Pennington, rented the lousiest accommodation I could find and got the job at the Mitre. All in the spirit of rebellion to punish my family for—for not being the family I thought they were.'

Joe's eyes blazed with scorn. 'I find it bloody hard to feel any sympathy. You played on mine like a virtuoso, with your sob story about your cruel cousin and your lack of friends. But you told me the absolute truth about one thing, Miss Dysart. You can be a real sweetheart when you try.'

Because she knew he was right Fen didn't argue, but every instinct urged her to run from the cold, cobalt stare and leave him to let himself out. Instead, when he showed no sign of departing, she told Joe she hadn't heard from Safehouse about the job.

'Which isn't Adam's fault, as I thought. He sent a reference off right away.' Fen gave him a cold little smile. 'You obviously forgot to put a word in for me. Don't worry. It doesn't matter.'

'I don't imagine it does now, but I didn't forget,' he said curtly. 'You'll hear in the morning.'

Fen suddenly wanted Joe to go so much she was ready to push him through the door she opened for him. 'Goodnight,' she said politely. 'Now you know the truth, and don't like me any more, there's no point in your hanging around.'

'I don't *like* you much at this moment,' Joe agreed, his eyes roving over her body with insolent familiarity. 'But the hell of it is, in spite of everything, I still want you.' He pulled her into his arms and kissed her fiercely, but Fen clamped her mouth shut in outrage and stood rigid and unresponsive until his arms fell away and he drew back, a pulse throbbing at the corner of his clenched mouth. 'Goodbye, then.'

Fen stared at him in stony silence, and after waiting a moment Joe turned on his heel and walked out. She closed the door, locked it, and because her legs had turned to rubber sat down at the table for a moment, wishing she could leave right that minute and go home to Friars Wood, where she belonged.

But there were things to do before she could shake the dust of 29 Farthing Street from her shoes. In the morning she would wait for the post, just in case there was something from Safehouse, then take the keys back to the rental company on her way to Stavely. In the meantime she would throw out the food she'd bought for a celebration meal with Joe, sort out her belongings and try to get some sleep.

Her smile was bleak as she took a last look through the clinically clean rooms on her way to bed. She was leaving the house in a far better state than she'd found it. A pity that the same cleaning-up process in her life had lost her Joe Tregenna. Always supposing he'd never been really hers in the first place. The high-flown bit about making love had been so much moonshine. It had been just basic old sex after all.

CHAPTER EIGHT

INSTEAD of a letter from Safehouse next morning Fen received a phone call from David Baker's assistant, asking her to come back for a second interview the following Monday. And, though Fen would have given much to tell the woman Safehouse could stuff their job, she agreed to the time suggested solely because she wanted to see Joe hard at work while she swept by on her way to her interview. After which, because rejection was new in her life, she'd avoid another by saying no thanks to David Baker before he said it first.

Fen made a couple of journeys to the car with luggage, television and microwave, then took down the curtains she'd bought and folded them into a bin liner with her cushions and bedlinen. At last she picked up the phone and rang Friars Wood.

'Gabriel?' she said, her voice suddenly breaking.

'*Fenny?* Oh, Fenny, I'm so glad to hear from you. I could have cried when Adam said you came here on Sunday to an empty house. Where are you now? When are you coming home?'

'Would right now be a bad time?' said Fen, swallowing tears in her relief.

'Of course not! Come right away. I'll ring Adam—no, I won't. We'll do a special dinner and surprise him tonight,' said Gabriel jubilantly, then paused, her voice troubled. 'You know, Fenny, I'd give the world—'

'Don't, Gabriel, please. Don't blame yourself. I had to know some time.'

'I just wish you hadn't found out from me.'

'And I wish I hadn't behaved like such a horrible brat and worried you so much. I'm desperately sorry. I've missed the boys so *much*. How are they—?' Fen broke off as she heard noisy crying in the background.

'That's how they are,' said Gabriel, laughing. 'You still want to come home?'

The warmth of Gabriel's welcome lightened Fen's mood considerably as she put the rest of her belongings in the car. She locked up for the last time, then with a sigh of relief turned her back on Farthing Street and drove to the rental agency to reclaim the deposit put down when she rented the house.

'No can do, love,' said the woman at the desk. 'You left the house before the time specified on the contract.'

'Will you tell your manager that Miss Dysart requires return of her deposit before he gets the keys to 29 Farthing Street?' said Fen, slapping down a receipt on the desk. 'Alternatively he can reimburse her for the new mattress she bought to replace the stained, insanitary disgrace provided by the company. His choice.'

Her tone sent the woman hurrying with the bill to the manager's office. When she returned almost immediately with a cheque Fen received it graciously, handed the keys over and swept out, well aware that it was the Dysart name, rather than her ultimatum, that had won the day.

On the drive back to Stavely Fen did her best to erase Joe Tregenna from her mind and concentrate on the joy of going home. She'd been away for longish periods before—to college, and on holidays with Laura, or to stay with Jess and Lorenzo in Florence—but no other homecoming had felt anything like as poignant as this one as she drove up the bends to Friars Wood.

In the Stables the decorators were hard at it, putting the finishing touches as she passed, preparing it for the return of her parents. Which, she realised, sniffing, was exactly what and who they were, no matter how stubbornly she'd refused to acknowledge it for the past month. Tom and Frances Dysart were the only parents she'd ever known and she was the luckiest person in the world to have them.

She was even reconciled by this time to the fact that her biological mother had been Rachel Dysart, Dad's much-loved sister. But the more recent revelation that Richard Savage was responsible for her existence was proving a lot harder to take on board.

The moment Fen cut the engine the front door flew open and Gabriel came hurrying down towards her, with Jamie in her arms and Hal and the dog hurtling past her in their rush to reach the car.

'Fenny, Fenny, where you been?' shouted Hal, beaming. 'Come and play.'

'I want a big, big kiss first,' said Fen, getting out. She patted the dog, then shooed him away to hold out her arms, and the little boy flew up into them, giving her a smacking wet kiss on her cheek. She hugged him, rubbed her cheek against his flaxen hair, then put him down to throw her arms round Gabriel, Jamie and all, and hold them tightly for a moment. 'The prodigal's back,' she said unsteadily.

'And about time, too, though I'm afraid we're all out of fatted calf,' said Gabriel, sniffing inelegantly. 'Leave your things for a bit, Fenny. Come inside and tell me all about this lover of yours.'

'What's a lover?' demanded Hal, swinging Fen's hand as they went up to the house, with Pan frisking behind.

'Someone who loves Fenny very much, like we do,' said his mother, thinking on her feet. She put her wriggling child down and held the dog by his collar. 'There you go, Jamie. Show Fenny your new trick.'

Jamie obediently tottered off down the hall for several unsteady steps before he plopped down on his rear outside the kitchen door, and beamed in triumph at his audience.

'Oh, *Jamie*,' said Fen, clapping. 'What a clever boy.'

'He can say words, too,' Hal informed her proudly.

'I've been away too long,' she said, clearing her throat.

'Much too long.' Gabriel pushed a strand of blonde hair behind one ear, then scooped Jamie up to take him into the big oblong kitchen, where windows looked out onto the garden and down on the Wye Valley far below. 'I still feel a bit like a visitor in here yet,' she said, filling a kettle. 'It's so big after the Stables.'

'But it was too much of a squeeze over there once Jamie arrived.' Fen leaned against the central island, which housed the electric hobs, provided counter space to work on, and otherwise served as resting place for the odds and ends of daily life that never found a home anywhere else.

'I know. But it was my first home with Adam,

so it was a bit of a wrench to leave it—even for a beautiful house like this.' Gabriel picked Jamie up and secured him in his highchair, and in response to imperious demands for juice handed him a lidded beaker and a biscuit, smoothed his feathery black curls, then sat Hal at the table with his own snack, and a colouring book and pencils. 'Darling, just stay there for a bit while I talk to Fenny. You'll get your turn in a minute.'

While Gabriel was seeing to her children Fen made coffee when the kettle boiled, added milk to both mugs and handed one over. 'Though I shouldn't be doing this. You're lady of the house now.'

'Don't be daft! Anyway, to me that title still belongs to Frances.' Gabriel's slate-blue eyes, deceptively sleepy to strangers, met Fen's head-on. 'And, while we're on the subject, what do we do about your little walkabout? Are you going to tell them?'

'Definitely. I've had it up to here with secrets.'

'If they had been the ones to put you in the picture, instead of me, would you have run off in the same way?'

Fen pulled a face. 'Knowing me, I might have.'

'Adam wanted to rush to bring you home the minute Tim contacted him, but I told him that if it were me I'd need time to come round.' Gabriel looked anxious. 'I just hope I didn't make things worse.'

'You did exactly the right thing. Horrible though it's been this last few weeks, I needed the time on my own to sort myself out.' Fen grinned. 'Did Adam tell you about the house I was living in?'

'It can't be as bad as he said, surely?'

'It's so gruesome I snapped it up the minute I saw it, just to get back at Adam. It's a student let—and it shows, believe me.'

'He went round there to inspect the place the moment he knew where you were. One look, even from the outside, and he was all for kidnapping you there and then, but thought better of it once he'd calmed down.' Gabriel cast a glance at her sons, but Hal was colouring away industriously and Jamie, covered in biscuit crumbs, seemed happy just watching him. 'Who is this lover of yours?' she asked in an undertone.

'Doesn't matter now. He's resigned the post,' said Fen, and heaved a deep, unsteady sigh. 'I'll never clean another window in my life.'

Gabriel's eyes widened. 'Explain!'

'When I thought Adam had refused a reference, I spring-cleaned the house to work off my temper. I even cleaned the windows, but I didn't shut the one in the kitchen properly, so when Joe arrived he was able to eavesdrop on my conversation with Adam, and just couldn't handle it.' Fen gave Gabriel a brief rundown on Joe Tregenna, then confessed her economy with the truth about her own background. 'Last night he heard me hurling filthy insults at Rachel, and found out that I was not a poor little orphan after all, but part of a large and loving family.'

'Are you in love with him, Fenny?' asked Gabriel with sympathy.

'Hopelessly so. But I'll get over it. Other fish in the sea and all that.' Fen jumped to her feet restlessly. 'Come on, then, Hal Dysart. Let's take Jamie out to play on the lawn.'

'When you come back I'll have lunch ready,' said Gabriel. 'And there are some postcards from far-away places for you, from Tom and Frances. Adam forgot to take them with him yesterday. They rang up a couple of times, so we lied through our teeth. Said your phone was broken and you were taking a break in London with Laura.'

When Adam returned home that night he found Fen helping his sons with their yacht race in the bath.

At the shrieks of welcome she turned round with a smile. 'Hi, "Daddy", I'm back.'

'Thank God for that.' Adam bent to ruffle her hair. 'The thought of you in that dump in Farthing Street was giving me nightmares.'

'Adam.' She looked up at him in appeal. 'It's

great to be home, but I'd better clear something up first as last. One thing my little adventure taught me is that it's time for me to stand on my own two feet. Mother and Dad won't like it, probably, but I'd really like a place of my own in town.'

'As long as it's something a whole lot better than Farthing Street I can live with that,' he assured her. 'So will they, when they get used to the idea.'

'Not that we want to get rid of you, but from my own experience I think it's a good thing,' said Gabriel, approaching with towels. 'Up you come, Jamie.'

'Daddy, Fen's got a lover,' said Hal confidentially.

Gabriel shot a guilty look at Fen, and handed a towel to Adam, who was trying desperately not to laugh. 'You can do Hal while I get Jamie dry. And,' she added, to no one in particular, 'I promise I will learn to keep my big mouth shut.'

'Your mouth isn't *big*, Mummy,' said Hal, holding up his arms to his father.

'Matter of opinion,' murmured Adam, rolling his eyes.

Fen grinned at him. 'I'll just go and tidy up before dinner. I'm soaked.'

In the room she'd slept in all her life, she stripped off her wet T-shirt and jeans, skewered her hair up in a knot, then took a quick shower before she allowed herself to check her cellphone. But there were no messages. From Joe or anyone else. When she was dressed she went along to the room the boys shared and volunteered to read bedtime stories while their parents snatched a few minutes to themselves. By the time she'd finished the third request both children were fast asleep.

Fen stood looking down at them for a moment or two, savouring the pleasure of being back home with them again. She blew the sleeping angels a silent kiss and went along to the master bedroom to report mission accomplished. And hurriedly backed out again at the sight of Adam and Gabriel locked in each other's arms.

'Don't go, Fen,' said Adam, grinning as he released his flushed wife. 'It's very quiet up here,' he added. 'Either you've beaten my sons into submission or they've gone to sleep.'

'You two may not have noticed the passage of time,' said Fen, fluttering her eyelashes, 'but I've been reading to them for half an hour. You bet they're asleep.'

Gabriel smiled gratefully, and went to check on her children, leaving Adam to talk with Fen.

'Are you really all right?' he asked immediately. 'Gabriel says you've broken up with Tregenna.'

'No. He broke up with me. He eavesdropped on us last night and heard things which turned him right off me.' Fen smiled valiantly. 'No matter.'

'If he's hurt you, Fenny, I'll beat him up!'

'Sweet of you, but if there's any beating up necessary I'll do it myself.'

'As usual! Come on then, tiger. If I can tear the light of my life away from our babies I'd quite like to eat.'

The weekend, which would have been intolerable in Farthing Street, passed as pleasantly as was currently possible for Fen in Friars Wood. Adam had kept his anxious sisters up to date with her escapade all along, but had sworn them to silence to let the runaway tell their parents about it herself when, or if, she could bring herself to do it.

'You'll have to, darling,' said Leonie practically, when Fen rang her. 'The parents are bound to hear you've been working in the Mitre, so bite the bullet and tell them first.'

'Will do.' Fen gave an odd little laugh. 'There's one good thing about all this, anyway. I made the amazing discovery that your husband is my cousin.'

Leonie chuckled. 'How do you feel about that?'

'Delighted.'

'Jonah always has been. Must rush; he's due home. See you soon, Fenny.'

Fen had a brief, very emotional chat with Jess in Florence, then a lengthier talk with Kate in Gloucester.

'It beats me how none of you ever let it slip before,' said Fen at one point.

'We never even thought of it. To us you've always been our baby sister,' said Kate simply.

Afterwards Fen wondered how she'd managed to go so long without talking to the trio who were in cold fact her cousins, but in warm reality the loving sisters who'd all taken a hand in bringing her up. And to make final peace with her world Fen rang Laura.

'I'm ringing to grovel,' she said without pre-amble, and half an hour later Fen put the phone down feeling a lot happier. Laura Green and Fen Dysart had been best friends since their first day at nursery school, and their rift had been so painful it was a huge relief to feel that in that area of her life, at least, things were back to normal.

To Adam's amusement, Fen was determined to turn up for the interview at Safehouse. Attired in her newest suit, she followed him into Pennington first thing on the Monday morning, and arrived to a warm reception from the staff. She spent a couple of hours settling into her cubbyhole next to Adam's office, then drove off to the Safehouse Insurance building mid-morning, wondering if Joe was the reason for her recall for a second interview. If so, it was a bit mystifying. She would have thought the last thing he wanted was even the chance of Fenella Dysart at work in the same building as him, however big it was. He would soon learn, thought Fen coldly, as she arrived there, that any intervention on his part had been unnecessary. She didn't need the job. She was back at Dysart's, where she belonged.

This time it was the pretty receptionist who escorted Fen up to the call centre, which was humming with its usual industry. Fen lagged behind as slowly as she dared so she could scan the room, but there was no sign of Joe Tregenna among the people manning the phones on the curving desks. So much for sweeping past in regal disdain, thought Fen, disappointed. If she'd known he wouldn't be here she wouldn't have bothered to come.

The receptionist led Fen past David Baker's office, and knocked on the door of the one next to it.

'Miss Dysart,' she announced, then withdrew, quietly closing the door behind her.

Fen's heart gave a sickening thump as a very familiar figure rose to his feet behind the desk, which immediately seemed a long way away, with miles of carpet to cross before she reached it.

'Good morning,' said Joe Tregenna pleasantly. He indicated the chair in front of his desk. 'Please sit down.'

Fen moved like an automaton and sat, crossing legs displayed to advantage by her short, narrow skirt.

'You're surprised,' said Joe, dragging his eyes away from them to look at her.

She nodded.

He smiled faintly. 'I kept my promise. I had a word with David Baker about you, but told him I'd conduct the second interview myself.'

'I see,' said Fen. She saw only too well. This was payback.

'Not,' Joe went on, 'that I imagine you're still interested in working here.'

'No, I'm not, thank you,' she said politely.

'Then why did you come?'

'Curiosity.'

'Even though you don't want or need the job?'

'Right.'

They looked at each other in stony silence. Fen determined to stare Joe out to the bitter end, but at last she got up. 'If there's nothing else—'

'Sit down, please,' he ordered, with such effortless authority Fen obeyed. 'Aren't you going to ask why I kept you in the dark about my job?'

'But you didn't.' She gave him a faint, frosted smile. 'You told me you sell insurance. Which you do.'

'Very successfully,' he agreed. 'The Pennington branch is my baby, but I founded the parent company with my brothers a few years ago. Something I intended telling you the night I got back, but in the circumstances I decided against it.'

'I see.' Fen looked at him curiously. 'Did you have some specific reason for keeping quiet about it beforehand?'

'Yes.' Joe sat back, relaxed. 'My money and my assets were the main attraction for Melissa, and one or two before her. So I decided to play it differently with you, and left out the bit about owning the company.' He shot a glittering look at her. 'Just as you gave the impression that your bar work was your only means of support.'

'It was at the time.'

'Was your motive similar to mine? To be valued for what rather than who you are?'

'Not at all.' Fen gave him an abrasive little smile. 'I always expect people to like me for myself. And so do you,' she added with sudden heat. 'All that stuff about wanting to be loved for yourself alone is so much rubbish. Once you saw the house in Farthing Street you were afraid I'd start asking for handouts if you told the truth.'

'You're wrong.' Joe's mouth tightened. 'Nor did I ask for anything as high-flown as love—'

'I know,' she said bitterly. 'Those lessons of yours were a real con. Because it was just sex after all.' She got up, eying him imperiously. 'By the way, purely from Mr Baker's point of view, was I successful in getting the job?'

'Yes.' He stood up and came round the desk.

'David was very impressed with you. But the last word on employee selection is mine.'

'Which in my case, of course, is no.'

'In view of our recent relationship it would have been no even if you were the friendless little orphan you made yourself out to be.'

Fen's eyes flashed. 'Not done for the big white chief to sleep with a mere employee.'

'Something like that,' he agreed, though something told her her barb had found its mark. 'But living with, rather than just sleeping with, was the impediment.'

'Awkward at the Christmas party,' Fen agreed, and raised an eyebrow. 'So why was I asked back today? A polite little letter in the post would have done—' She slapped a dramatic hand to her forehead. 'Of *course*. Silly me. You wanted me to know that you're the top banana, not just one of the bunch.'

'Ignoble though it is, yes,' he said without compunction.

'Right. Consider me impressed, Mr Tregenna.'

The look he gave her made Fen uneasy.

'One thing, before you go. Why did you lie to me about your family?'

She shrugged. 'Just like you, I didn't actually lie. At the time I was still in shock after learning the truth about my birth. Not that I could have told you the whole truth, anyway. Until Adam came to

Farthing Street last week I didn't even know all of it myself.' She gave him a sudden steely look. 'I assume I can trust you to keep what you heard to yourself?'

'If you need to ask that,' he said curtly, 'it's pointless for me to answer.'

'I'll take that as a yes, then. Now, I'm sure you're a very busy man, so I'll say goodbye.' Fen aimed a meaningless little smile somewhere over Joe's shoulder and set off across the expanse of carpet towards the door. But he was there before her, barring her way, and to her outrage caught her in his arms, his mouth crushing hers for an instant.

'Goodbye, Fen,' he said, releasing her. 'Or are you Fenny again?'

'Of course.' And instead of punching him on the nose, as she so badly wanted to, she gave him a cold, insolent little smile. 'But only to my nearest and dearest.'

CHAPTER NINE

FEN was confident that she would get over Joe Tregenna once she was living at home again and fully involved in her old job at Dysart's. With an important auction looming, she stayed on most nights after her own work was finished, eager to make reparation to Adam by helping out as much as she could. And to tire herself out enough to sleep at night.

Turning up for the unnecessary interview had been a bad mistake. After seeing Joe again none of the frenetic activity was any use at combating the dull ache of loss now he was gone from her life. By day, and even in the evenings, with Gabriel and Adam, she was able to pretend the ache wasn't there. But at night, alone in bed, she was helpless against the anguish of it. And the worst thing, she realised miserably, was missing him as a friend, not just a lover. Though she missed that part, too. To a humiliating extent some nights. But she'd loved just being in Joe's company in a way she never had with any other man outside her family.

Tom and Frances Dysart were due back the following week, an event Fen was looking forward to with mixed feelings. She longed to see them again, but at the same time quailed at the thought of telling them she knew the truth about her birth. She was coming to terms with it by this time, but behind her confident exterior lurked a new vulnerability made all the worse by the split with Joe Tregenna. Sometimes she felt as though her entire world wobbled on its foundations. She swore Adam and Gabriel to silence about her brief love affair. There was more than enough emotive clearing up to do with her parents without bringing Joe into the equation.

Tom and Frances were arriving from a stay in Florence with Jess and Lorenzo on the following Saturday. They would spend a few days in London with Leonie and Jonah, in Hampstead, then travel down to Stavely. Which meant a hectic weekend coming up for the loved ones on site, to make the Stables ready for occupation by the time their parents arrived home. Frances had given her son a list of the furniture she wanted transferred from the main house, and Adam had roped in Mrs Briggs, the housekeeper, to come up for a few extra hours to look after the boys while the rest of them got both houses in order.

Over dinner shortly before the auction there was a conference to decide how to go about the change-over.

'The best thing,' said Gabriel, 'would be to put furniture in obvious places easy to change if Frances wants to.'

'Which she will,' said Adam with certainty. 'We'll hang curtains and put a few ornaments around, so it doesn't look bare, but no pictures until she says where they're to go.'

'She'll have Dad there with a hammer and picture hooks for hours,' said Fenny, chuckling, and looked up to see Adam exchanging a look with Gabriel. 'What?'

'It's the first time you've actually said "Dad",' Adam informed her, and passed a vegetable dish. 'Have some more. You look a bit skinny.'

'Thanks a lot!' Fen helped herself to a potato. 'Talking of my personal charms, I was so mad at you when you got me sacked from the Mitre that I searched the papers for a job you'd hate even more.' She gave him an evil grin. 'Pole-dancing in some tawdry club was the post of choice.'

Gabriel roared with laughter. 'I can just see Adam's face at the sight of his little sister twined round a pole, wearing a few beads in strategic places—'

'What the hell would I be doing in a place like that?' demanded her husband irately, then paused to consider. 'Not that I know of one in Pennington.'

'Even if there were any,' said Fen with a sigh, 'my strategic places, as Gabriel puts it, aren't really the kind required for the job.'

'You jerked my chain hard enough just by singing on top of a piano at the Mitre,' said Adam, shuddering. 'But the thought of pole-dancing—'

'They do it for the aerobic benefits in some health clubs,' Gabriel informed him demurely. 'I wonder if any of the clubs in Pennington offer anything like that? I could do with getting my figure back in shape since Jamie put paid to it.'

'Over my dead body,' said Adam wrathfully. 'Your shape suits me very well just the way it is, Gabriel Dysart. So no pole-dancing. For either of you,' he added.

'OK,' said his wife meekly, and smiled enviously at Fen. 'You don't need it, love, anyway.'

'I will soon if I don't get back into my regular running schedule.'

'You'll get plenty of exercise at the weekend, just lugging furniture around,' Adam promised, and gave her a straight look. 'It might make you sleep better, too. With those marks under your eyes Mother will think I've been working you into the ground.'

* * *

There was a good crowd in the auction rooms on the viewing day before the sale. Fen stayed at her desk most of the morning, but just before lunch she went down to mingle with the crowd to find out which lots were attracting the most interest. In her jeans and T-shirt, with her nose in a catalogue, she was indistinguishable from the rest, except to some of the dealers.

Fen loved to try and gauge which items would sell for the most, and a big auction like this would be in three stages. First Adam would auction off the smaller, affordable objects—none of them particularly rare, but all of them interesting. She made a note to tell him that the lots winning several return visits from viewers included a pair of needlework footstools, an alabaster group of children, and—her own favourite—a Victorian girandole with the original mirror framed in gilded cast-iron.

The more expensive section offered a diamond bow brooch and a boxed set of Georgian silver tea caddies among the mouthwatering goodies Adam hoped would attract enthusiastic bidding. But his main love was the selection of paintings and drawings hung on the damson-red walls, and the art sale was always the climax of the day.

'Good crowd in,' she reported, when she went up to Adam's office.

'Let's hope they all come back tomorrow.'

'Of course they will. There was a lot of studied nonchalance in front of your pictures,' said Fen, grinning. 'I know the cottage garden watercolours always go like hot cakes, but what's the hot tip for the day?'

'Who knows?' Adam stretched mightily. 'There's a couple of Edwardian London scenes—oils on wood—that should do well, some good sepia drawings, Caulfield lithographs, and so on.'

'But which one do you fancy?'

'A while ago I found an oil of a young boy by an unknown artist. Harry Brett restored it for me, and says it was definitely painted around 1800, but he can't find a signature. He says Dutch, but though it's bad manners to disagree with my father-in-law it speaks with a Scottish accent to me—though maybe not Sir David Wilkie.' Adam tapped his nose. 'Something tells me it should do well, whoever painted it. And there's a Patrick Heron print which should do the same. Prices for his work are on the up since his death a couple of years ago.' He smiled at her. 'Fancy sitting with me on the rostrum tomorrow? You can make sure I don't miss anyone.'

'As if you would! But I'd love that, Adam.' Fen's eyes shone as she reached to kiss his cheek. 'Thanks for having me back, spoilt brat though I am.'

He put his arm round her. 'Still hurts?'

'Truth does,' she said sadly.

Next day an even bigger crowd gathered in the auction rooms for the actual sale, and Fen took her place alongside Adam with a feeling of intense anticipation, hoping her appearance lived up to Adam's elegance. Putting the last time she'd worn it from her mind, she'd chosen the black trouser suit to contrast with the red walls, swept her hair up in a knot and wore pearl drops in her ears.

'Nice look,' murmured Adam as he took his place beside her. He smiled at the crowd, a porter held up the first lot, Adam described it in glowing terms, and the bidding was off to a brisk start.

At first Fen's concentration was absolute, but after a while she relaxed and settled down, enjoying herself as most of the items surpassed their estimates by gratifying amounts. After the diamond bow brooch she'd fancied went for more than three times the forecast she grinned ruefully at Adam.

'I was hoping to get that in my Christmas stocking.'

'Fond hope,' he muttered. 'Right. Here we go. Fine Art section coming up.'

The sale went well, right up to the moment when Fen spotted Joe Tregenna in the crowd. She looked through him without recognition, keeping her attention on the bidding while Adam's unsigned

painting went for a good price to a telephone
bidder. But after Joe bought the Heron for twice as
much as expected Fen could take no more.

'Adam,' she whispered, 'could you manage on
your own now? There's only a couple more lots to
go.'

'Yes, of course. Nasty surprise to see Tregenna?'

'I could have done without it, but at least he paid
a good price for the Heron.'

Fen descended from her perch with a smile for
the porter, who helped her down. She left the sale
room unobtrusively, and flew upstairs to the safety
of her office, furious because she'd been panicked
into retreat by the insolent cobalt eyes mocking her
from the far side of the room.

Adam put his head round the door later, looking concerned. 'You look done in, Fenny. Why
not take off now? It's all over, but I'll be a while
yet.'

She smiled at him gratefully. 'I will, boss, if you
don't mind. Good day, I thought. Your painting did
well.'

'Not bad at all,' he agreed with satisfaction. 'See
you later.'

Because Adam often stayed late, or had other
things on in the evening before he went home,
Fen drove herself into Pennington every day—
something she was deeply thankful for right then.
Until she reached the Dysart car park and found

Joe Tregenna leaning against her car, wearing the chalk-striped grey suit of the interview, which still gave her the horrors every time she thought of it. Which was most of the time.

'Hello, Fenny,' he said, infuriating her before he said another word.

She looked at him, unsmiling. 'This is a private car park.'

'My car isn't here.'

'But you are. So if you'd just move away, I'd like to drive home.'

When Joe showed no immediate signs of complying Fen stared at him with hauteur and took her cellphone from her bag. 'If you don't move I'll ring—'

'The police?' He smiled and straightened up. 'A bit extreme. And ungrateful, when I came out of my way to return your property.'

'Adam, not the police,' she said crisply. 'He offered to beat you up for me, by the way.'

'Why should he want to do that?' said Joe with interest. 'I paid a damn good price for the print.'

'Oh, please,' said Fen wearily. 'You're obviously enjoying this, but I'm not. Which I assume is the object of the exercise. So, unless you want me to call a couple of porters to remove you, just stand away from my car.'

'I thought you might want this.' Joe slid a hand

into his inside jacket pocket and to her outrage
produced a black lace bra. 'Or am I wrong?' he
enquired, dangling it from a forefinger. 'It's the
right size, as far as I can remember, but it could
well be someone else's.'

For answer Fen began punching buttons on her
phone, but Joe seized it from her to switch it off.
'This is between you and me, Fen, nothing to do
with your cousin, or brother, or whatever you call
him these days.'

'There's nothing between you and me any more,
either,' she said tightly. 'So stop fooling about and
let me pass.'

'First,' he said, all trace of humour gone from
his eyes, 'I'd like to know something.'

'What?'

'How old you are, for a start.'

She stared at him blankly. 'What possible interest can my age be to you?'

'Indulge me.'

'Twenty-two,' she snapped.

Joe nodded slowly. 'I suppose that accounts for
it.'

'What do you mean?'

He smiled, and Fen wished he hadn't. 'The spoilt
brat syndrome.'

'How old are you?' she demanded.

'Almost ten years older, but not much wiser,

unfortunately.' His mouth twisted. 'If I were I'd have run a mile the first time we met.'

'Make up for it now. Take off. I'm not keeping you.'

Joe looked at her for a moment, then held out the fragment of lace. 'It is yours, Fen.'

'I know.'

'As a matter of interest, there was no possibility of it belonging to anyone else,' he said without inflection.

'It isn't. Of interest, I mean.' Which was a lie. The mere thought of anyone else shedding underwear in his flat cut her to pieces.

'That just about wraps it up, then,' said Joe casually.

'Yes. Goodbye.' Fen moved towards him, sure he would give way, but she was wrong. Instead of stepping aside Joe pulled her into his arms and kissed her so forcefully she bit his lip in knee-jerk reaction.

Cursing, he dodged away, a hand to his mouth, and Fen snatched the bra from him, tucked it into her bag and took out a tissue. 'Use this or you'll ruin your suit.'

Joe dabbed at his lip, watching as she unlocked the car. 'It went wrong,' he said abruptly.

She raised an eyebrow as she slid into the driver's seat. 'What did?'

'I came here to buy something for the flat,

curious to see if I'd catch a glimpse of you. I didn't
bargain for the sight of you up there with Adam,
wearing the suit I remember so well. You looked
so poised and pleased with yourself.' He glared at
her. 'Which you should be, Fenella Dysart. One
look at you today and I wanted to snatch you down
from your perch and punch the porter who laid a
hand on you.'

Fen stared incredulously. 'Are you sure you've
got the right female? This is the spoilt brat you're
talking to.'

'I know,' Joe said in disgust, and ran the tip of
his tongue gingerly over his split lip. 'And, bloody
fool that I am, I still want you.'

'Tough!' She switched on the ignition, shot out
of the car park, and narrowly missed collision with
another car as she reached the road. Cursing Joe
Tregenna with vocabulary which would have made
Frances Dysart blench, Fen drove back to Stavely
at twice her usual speed, oblivious of police cam-
eras along the route in her haste to get home.

After changing into jeans, it took a good half-
hour spent playing with the boys and Pan on the
lawn before Fen felt normal. After a while Jamie
said, 'Mum-Mum?' so imperiously that Fen smiled
and picked him up. Then, taking Hal by the hand,
she whistled for Pan and took her charges up one
of the stone stairways leading from the lawn to the

terrace, entering the house just as Gabriel came running downstairs to meet them.

'For you, Mummy,' said Hal, handing her a daisy.

'How lovely. Thank you, darling.' Gabriel kissed him, smiling gratefully at Fen as she took Jamie. 'It was great to have a leisurely bath for once. Your turn now, love. You look tired.'

'Busy day.' Fen stretched, yawning. 'But very successful for Dysart's.'

'Not for you?'

'No. Joe was there.'

'Wow!'

'Who's Joe?' said Hal, tugging at Fen's hand.

'A man I used to know,' she told him. 'He bought a picture from Daddy.'

Gabriel eyed her sharply. 'I'll talk to you later,' she said with meaning, and put Jamie down to crawl upstairs in front of her. 'Come on, Hal. Bath time.'

During dinner, which was more festive than usual to celebrate the success of the auction, Adam got up to answer the phone and returned, smiling, beckoning to Fen.

'Someone for you.'

'Who?'

'Go and see.'

Sure it was Joe, Fen raced along the hall to pick up the phone. 'Hello?' she said breathlessly.

'Darling, how are you?' said Frances Dysart, and Fen slid to the floor in a heap.

'Oh, *Mummy*, I've missed you so much!'

When Fen went back to the table later, Gabriel looked at her tear-stained face with concern. 'You didn't tell Frances right away?'

'No fear. But once I heard her voice I got a bit emotional. She wouldn't talk long because it's Lorenzo's phone.'

'I doubt that Lorenzo grudges Mother a few lira on his phone bill,' said Adam.

'Dad wouldn't let her talk any longer,' said Fen, and smiled guiltily. 'I think I worried her, though. I called her Mummy.'

'That must have thrown her! You informed her that Mummy was too childish when you were about nine,' Adam reminded her.

'Little darling that I was! It just slipped out the minute I heard her voice.' And because it was Joe's voice she'd been hoping to hear. 'Anyway, Tuesday's crunch time, folks, so we've got four full days to get things straight.'

'All the paint's dry in the Stables,' said Gabriel. 'Mrs Briggs went through afterwards with a vacuum cleaner, and she'll be back tomorrow, bright and early, to look after the boys.'

'Isn't she getting on a bit for cleaning?' said Fen. 'She's been doing it for ever.'

'She likes to come—says it gets her out of the house. And she only puts in two days a week now. If anything special's going on she enlists her daughters.'

After dinner Fen looked out at the late sunshine streaming through the kitchen windows, and felt restless. 'I think I'll take Pan for a nice long walk— maybe as far as the farm for once.'

'Missing your run?' said Gabriel.

'I'll get back to it once I'm set in my routine again. In the meantime I need exercise.'

Fen took Pan's lead from the hook, and with difficulty, because he was frisking around like a puppy, clipped it to his collar. 'All right, all right, we're going. See you later,' she called to the others, and set off with a feeling she identified after a while as escape.

She felt ungrateful. It was wonderful to be back home, but after the enforced period of living alone she found it strangely restricting to be in the constant company of others again. It wasn't fair on Adam and Gabriel, either. It was time she found a flat in Pennington. Rachel Dysart, she knew, had left Stavely and Friars Wood when the time was right, just as Leo, Kate and Jess had done in turn, so her own urge to fly the nest was long overdue. Fen strode down the lane which led past the farm. For the first time she was able to think of Rachel objectively, as a mother who'd entrusted her baby to the people she knew would love her as their own. But if Rachel really had died of a broken heart it was vital to build a shell round her own, decided Fen, to make sure she never lost it to anyone again.

When she got back to the house she gave Pan a couple of his favourite biscuits, refilled his water bowl, then went along to the study with him to announce she was off to bed.

'This early?' said Adam suspiciously. 'You're not going up there to sob into your pillow, by any chance?'

'No. I'm going to collapse on my bed and watch my own little television, and give you people some space,' Fen said bluntly.

'You don't have to—' began Gabriel, then smiled. 'But maybe you could do with a little space of your own.'

'Come back down if you get bored with it,' ordered Adam, in a tone so peremptory Fen knew it hid anxiety.

'I will,' she promised. 'Shall I look in on the boys?'

'No fear!' Gabriel smiled. 'If they wake up they'll be pestering you for more stories.'

An hour later Fen was propped up in bed, trying to interest herself in a courtroom drama, when Gabriel hurried in. She handed over a cellphone and a scrap of paper. 'Your Mr Tregenna wants you to ring him on this number. Apparently it's urgent. Adam said use his.'

'I have no intention of ringing Joe Tregenna, and even if I did I can use my own phone,' said Fen, leaping out of bed.

Gabriel grinned and went out, closing the door softly behind her.

Fen was still scowling at the familiar number Adam had scribbled down when the phone in her hand rang, startling her. Ready to apologise for not being Adam, she sat down abruptly at the sound of Joe's voice.

'Fen, don't ring off,' he ordered.

'What do you want?' she said brusquely.

'To see you.'

'Why?'

'To apologise for my behaviour this afternoon, for one.'

'No need to see me for that.'

'I want to return something to you.'

'If it's any more underwear, keep it as a souvenir!'

'I meant your phone. You took off in such a hurry I didn't give it back.'

Fen ground her teeth. 'I hadn't even missed it. I wondered how you had Adam's mobile number.'

'When can we meet?'

'We don't have to meet. You can send the phone to Dysart's and leave it with one of the porters.'

'I prefer to hand it over in person.'

Fen made him wait a while. 'Oh, very well,' she said at last.

'I'll take you to lunch tomorrow—'

'No, you won't. I'll just meet you for a minute in my lunch hour. One o'clock in the park, near the statue of Queen Victoria.'

'Which park?'

'Victoria Park, of course,' she said impatiently. 'If you're not there on the dot I won't wait.'

'I will be. And thank Adam for me,' he added, surprising her.

'What for?'

'Acting as a very unwilling go-between just now. It took a lot of persuasion on my part.'

'I bet it did. Goodnight.' Fen pressed the 'off' button and went downstairs to return Adam's phone.

'What did he want?' demanded Adam.

'He's got my phone.'

'I saw you tucking it in your bag before you went out this morning,' said Gabriel, surprised. 'How come he's got it?'

Fen curled up in her father's chair and, leaving out the kiss, described the incident in the auction house car park.

'You should have seen her when she noticed Tregenna,' Adam told his wife. 'She went white.'

'Which is quite a trick for someone with skin

tone like mine,' said Fen, deliberately flippant. 'All right. It gave me a bit of a turn. But it won't again. Joe and I both work in Pennington, so we're bound to run into each other now and then. I'll be a big girl and take it in my stride next time. Which is tomorrow, by the way. I'm meeting him in Victoria Park to get my phone back.'

Adam frowned. 'I'd better come with you—'

'You will not,' said Gabriel. 'Let her sort it out herself.'

'Yes, ma'am,' said Adam, saluting, and gave Fen a questioning look. 'Tregenna paid quite a sum for that print today by the time he'd coughed up buyer's premium on top of hammer price. You said he sells insurance for these Safehouse people, but does his job pay that well?'

'He's a co-founder of the company. He set up Safehouse Insurance with his brothers in London, then came here to run the branch when they expanded.'

The other two stared at her.

'The day you went for interview, Fenny,' said Gabriel slowly, 'you were very quiet afterwards.'

'Mr Tregenna was playing a little game. He set me up for a second interview just so he could have me brought to his office and show me quite literally who was boss.' Fen shrugged. 'Retaliation. He was angry with me for what he called my sob-story about my background.'

'He was keeping you in the dark about his at the same time,' said Adam sharply. 'Why?'

'Apparently he wanted to be loved for the beauty of his nature rather than for his financial assets.' Fen scowled. 'But *I* think he took one look at the house in Farthing Street and decided I'd start sponging if I knew he was loaded.'

'But you say his flat is in Chester Square. It costs the earth to live there. Didn't you wonder about that?'

'Of course I did. He told me he had a crippling mortgage.'

'It must have been a shock for you that day, when you went for interview and found he was running the outfit,' said Gabriel with feeling.

'You bet it was.' Fen grimaced. 'I was so wired up afterwards I would have howled if I'd try to tell you about it.'

'Are you sure you don't want me to beat him up?' growled Adam.

'Think of the headlines!'

'"Adam Dysart Socks Sister's Seducer",' agreed Gabriel, pulling a face. She wagged a finger at her husband. 'So no trailing Fenny to the park tomorrow.'

'Right.' Adam grinned. 'But even if I did, Tregenna's a shade on the hefty side for any beating up.'

* * *

Just before one the following day Fen left the auction house and strolled to the park. In carefully chosen denim skirt and sleeveless shirt, denim jacket over her shoulders and flat sandals on her bare feet, she blended in well with the crowd seeking fresh air and sunshine. As she neared the statue she checked her watch, to make sure she'd arrived a full five minutes late, then saw Joe leaning against one of the ornamental lamp posts lining the walkways. He was in his shirtsleeves, his suit jacket slung over one shoulder and a brown paper bag in the other hand. And her heart did a somersault in her chest at the sight of him.

He straightened, smiling in surprise as she approached. 'I didn't recognise you at first. I was expecting the efficient Miss Dysart in city suit. You look like a schoolgirl in that gear.'

'Are you the kind who fantasises over such things?' she returned.

'No, I bloody well am not,' he retorted, then breathed in deeply. 'Let's start again. Hello, Fen.'

'Hello. Have you got my phone?'

'Not so fast. Let's walk.'

'I haven't got long.'

He raised a sardonic eyebrow. 'I doubt that Adam docks your wages if you're late back from lunch.'

'Of course not. Which doesn't mean I'll spend my hour off with you,' Fen informed him.

'Why not?' he demanded, beginning to stroll, and because she wanted her phone back she was forced to fall in step.

'We're no longer friends,' she pointed out.

Joe glanced at her. 'I regret that.'

So did she. If she were honest Fen knew that there was nothing she wanted more, right this moment, than a walk in the park with Joe Tregenna. 'You found Queen Victoria, then.' Wonderful. Top marks for inanity.

'No misleading road signs on the way this time,' he said. 'Let's go this way.' He turned down a less-frequented path which led to a shaded spot by the river, as Fen knew well, but she was surprised that Joe did.

'I did some research beforehand,' he informed her, reading her mind.

'Once more I'm impressed.'

Joe was quiet for a moment. 'I shouldn't have done that.'

'Done what?'

'Called you back for an interview just so I could show off. Though in my own defence I never dreamed you'd turn up.'

'I came purely in the hope of seeing you grafting away at one of those desks, while I stalked past in disdain,' she said frankly. 'After that I was going to tell David Baker to stuff his job and go back where I belonged. For good.'

'Instead you got mauled by the boss for your pains.' Joe's mouth twisted in wry distaste. 'I wonder you didn't have me up for sexual harassment.'

'It never occurred to me,' she said with regret. 'What an opportunity I missed.'

'You could always come back and let me do it again.'

'If I let you, it wouldn't be harassment.'

'True. Let's find some shade,' Joe suggested. 'How about that tree over there?'

'Good choice. I know this spot well. Laura and I used to bring our cheeseburgers to eat along here on Saturday afternoons after the cinema. They tasted wonderful because they were forbidden fruit,' Fen informed him, smiling. 'My mother disapproves of fast food. I used to pack wet wipes to mop up afterwards, so she couldn't smell it on me.'

Joe laughed, and held out his jacket. 'Sit on this.'

'Good heavens, no. My skirt will suffer a lot less than your suit jacket. And the ground's dry.' Fen sat down, long bare legs outstretched.

'I can't rise to cheeseburgers, but I've brought lunch,' said Joe, offering her the brown bag as he sat beside her. 'Will you share it with me?'

She eyed it in surprise. 'What is it?'

'Take a look.'

Fen took out two packets of sandwiches. 'Crab,' she said huskily.

'Which took a while to find,' he assured her, and opened one of the packs. 'I forgot to bring napkins this time.'

Fen took a pack of tissues from her bag. 'Have one of these.'

'What a resourceful girl you are!'

'Some of my sex object to the term girl,' she pointed out, and took a bite of her sandwich.

'But that's what you are,' said Joe. 'Just a girl, Fen. Especially today. You look very young in that get-up.'

'Then I must wear it more often.' She gave him a covert look, liking the way his hair lifted in the breeze from the river, how his face looked dark in the shade against the white of his shirt. She turned away quickly and went on with the sandwich.

'You also look tired,' said Joe. 'Adam working you too hard?'

'No. There's been a lot going on at Dysart's. It's all hands on deck at auction time.'

He finished his sandwich and got up to dip a handful of tissues in the river. He mopped his hands, then walked back to her, smiling, and hunkered down to offer her a fresh wodge of damp tissue. 'Will this do instead of wet wipes?'

'Perfectly. Thank you.' Fen scrubbed her mouth and hands, afraid to look into the face which was so near to hers she could feel the heat from his skin.

'Don't worry,' he said softly. 'I'm not going to kiss you again. For one thing this is a public place—'

'A pity you didn't think of that yesterday in our car park,' she retorted.

'Which is the other thing. My lip is too sore for kisses after your treatment. Unless,' he added softly, leaning nearer, 'you'd like to kiss it better.'

'Not really,' she lied.

'Pity.' He looked at her closely as he sat down again. 'Just now, Fen, you mentioned your mother so naturally I assume you've come to terms with the facts of your birth.'

'More or less. Though I'm not looking forward to telling my parents I know about it.' She shivered. 'Nor to owning up to what happened next.'

'Will you tell them about me?' Joe asked, surprising her.

'No point in that.'

'Which puts me in my place.'

Fen's eyes, pure green under the trees, turned on him thoughtfully. 'What else did you expect? You didn't care for the real Fenella Dysart at all, so you took off. End of story.'

Joe shook his head. 'It's not.'

'Yes, it is. You won't get the chance to hurt me twice.' In one lithe movement she got to her feet. 'Time I went back to work.'

Joe got up with equal ease, and picked up his jacket. 'I'll walk back with you.'

'No need.'

'I'm not letting you walk this section of park alone, even at this time of day.'

'Joe,' she said impatiently. 'I run along the stretch of river farther along all the time.'

'I know. It worries me.'

'Why?'

By mutual consent they halted, facing each other.

His eyes darkened. 'You know damn well why.'

'I don't need someone to watch over me any more, Joe. Not that I ever did, really,' she added.

His mouth compressed. 'In other words I should have driven past that night and left you to fight your own battle.'

'No,' said Fen honestly. 'I'm glad you didn't, even if it did end in tears. So let's part on an amicable note this time. Thank you for lunch.'

'Don't mention it,' he said savagely, and screwed the brown bag into a ball to shy it into one of the park's ornamental wastebins as they passed.

'We could walk as far as the gate together,' she offered, secretly in no hurry to part from Joe.

He shook his head. 'I'll see you safe back to Dysart's.'

Which Fen regretted when Adam emerged from it as they arrived together.

'Hello,' he said, surprised. 'What are you doing here?'

'Bringing your sister back,' said Joe stiffly.

'Actually, I meant Fenny,' said Adam. 'She's supposed to take the afternoon off.'

Such bright scarlet colour suffused her face both men stared at it, riveted.

'I thought you were in a hurry to get back,' Joe said to her, in a tone neither Fen nor Adam cared for very much.

'I don't make her clock in and out,' said Adam curtly, and glanced at his watch. 'I must be off. I'm due in Cirencester. Go home, Fenny. Rest up before the weekend.' He nodded to Joe and went off to his car, leaving a taut silence between the two people watching as he drove from the car park.

'What's happening this weekend?' asked Joe at last.

'We're getting things shipshape before my parents get back, which is why I'm taking time off this afternoon.'

'If you're skiving off maybe I will too,' said Joe, and handed Fen her phone. He gave her a look which stopped her heart for an instant. 'Will you come home with me for a while? Just for tea,' he added, 'not love in the afternoon—'

'Love?' retorted Fen. 'Call a spade a spade, Mr Tregenna. It was just basic sex.'

CHAPTER TEN

THE picnic by the river with Joe stopped Fen's recovery programme in its tracks. A mere half-hour in his company had made it cruelly clear how much she missed talking to him, just being with him. So much so that on the drive back to Stavely she almost turned back to take him up on his invitation. Even if it meant saying yes to more than tea and cakes. But common sense pointed out that Joe Tregenna would be back at his grand executive desk at Safehouse by that time, and she would do better to have tea with Gabriel and the boys.

'I'll be glad to have my big brass bed back,' said Adam next morning, while Fen helped him manouevre the heavy headrest up the stairs. He leered down at Gabriel, who was following behind with a small table. 'It has very fond associations for me.'

'Do I want to know about this?' panted Fen. 'Watch it—you'll mark the wall.'

'He means,' said Gabriel demurely, 'that it was where he first seduced me.'

Fen grinned over her shoulder. 'How did he go about the seduction bit?'

'Plied me with pizza and videos one rainy evening while his mother and father were away.'

'Cheapskate,' said Fen, unimpressed.

'It worked like a charm,' Adam assured her.

'Novelty value, darling,' Gabriel said sweetly. 'I was accustomed to London restaurants at the time. It was the rustic contrast that swept me off my feet.'

Remembering the same kind of evening with Joe, Fen could well believe it. 'Keep going, Adam. Right hand down a bit.'

'Are you sure you're all right with this, Fenny?' he asked. 'I could have got some of the lads in to help—'

'And have them tramping all over Mother's new carpet? No fear. I'm glad to help. Lord knows I've got nothing better to do.'

By late Sunday evening the exchange of furniture was complete, both houses immaculate, and the Stables ready for Frances Dysart's finishing touches.

'She'll probably have Dad lugging furniture around for hours before she's satisfied,' said Adam, yawning. 'Lord, I hope number two son sleeps a bit better tonight.' He exchanged a look with his wife. 'When I got my brass bed back the plan was *not* to share it with Jamie.'

Fen chuckled. 'Send him in to me tonight, if you like.'

'Time for that when you've got one of your own, Fenny.'

She sobered. 'That's not going to happen any time soon. If ever.'

'It will,' said Gabriel firmly. 'I was over thirty when I met Adam. You're a mere babe.'

'Babe is right,' said Adam, eyeing Fenny's shorts and bare midriff. 'A good thing you don't come to work like that. As the only thing keeping the junior porters in hand is fear of the boss.'

'Do they fancy me, then?' said Fen, much cheered.

'If your name were anything other than Dysart you'd be beating them off with a stick!'

Fen went off to bed, tired after her hard day's labour but pleased by Adam's careless compliments. Then, as she got ready for bed, it struck her that only a few short weeks before her self-esteem wouldn't have needed such bolstering. But the revelation about her birth, coupled with the brief, stormy relationship with Joe Tregenna, had wrought personality changes which promised to be permanent.

Fen met a pair of brooding eyes in the mirror as she brushed her hair. She had told the truth

about children of her own. With Joe ruled out as
the father she preferred to sublimate any maternal
feelings in the role of favourite aunt. As Rachel
had until she'd met the only love of her life. Fen
sighed. In the past when she'd sent yet another
boyfriend packing her sisters had assured her she'd
know the right one when she found him, because
the Dysart females were all one-man women. A
genetic quirk to Kate the scientist, but the Dysart
legacy to Leo and Jess. Fen had jeered at the time,
but knew exactly what they meant now she'd met
Joe.

But during the next two days any thoughts of
Joe Tregenna were pushed to the back of her mind
by the confession looming over her joy at seeing
her parents again. Fen planned to go home early
to shower and change on the day, to be ready and
waiting the minute their car appeared up the drive.
But to her annoyance Adam kept her later than
usual, insisting that she type up the inventory of a
clearance he'd been to the day before.

'Don't worry, we'll get home in good time,' he
told her later, as she thrust the finished inventory
in front of him. 'But I'll go first.'

'Why?'

'So you don't get done for speeding on the way
back to Stavely. Come on. I'll leave Reg Parker to
lock up.'

To Fen's frustration Adam kept to the exact legal

limit at every stage on the twenty-mile journey to Friar's Wood. She was at screaming point by the time she turned up the drive. Then she saw two familiar cars parked in front of the main house and shot from her own to race along the terrace to the tall, grey-haired man holding out his arms.

'Dad!' Fen hurled herself at him and he hugged her close, kissed her, then passed her on to his wife.

'Fenny, darling.' Frances held her at arm's length after repeating the process. 'Just look at you! Adam's obviously been working you too hard—'

'I knew you'd say that,' said her son, arriving for his own kiss. 'Hi, folks, had a good time?'

'Wonderful,' said Tom Dysart. 'How's business?'

'Stop that,' ordered his wife. 'No shop-talk tonight. We're celebrating.'

Fen took in a deep breath. 'I've got something to tell you first—'

'Hi, Fenny, you're late,' interrupted Leonie Savage, hurrying out to kiss her.

'Leo!' said Fen joyfully, hugging her sister, who, give or take a few silver hairs and laughter lines, was even more stunning in her forties than in her youth. Leonie patted Fen's cheek and passed her into the arms of the man waiting behind her.

'Don't worry, princess,' Jonah Savage whispered

in Fen's ear, then gave way to his small nephew, who was demanding Fen's attention in turn.

'Sorry, Hal,' she apologised, and took his hand to ask about his day before she turned back to her mother, who looked tanned and rested, her grey curling hair cut short in a new style. 'Trendy!'

'Had it done in Florence,' said Frances, pleased, and began shooing her tribe to the kitchen. 'We're very rude, hanging about out here while Gabriel and Mrs Briggs slave away in the kitchen.'

Showdown postponed until later, Fen surrendered Hal to Gabriel, who told her to move it if she wanted a shower because the meal would be ready in half an hour.

'On my way. I had hoped to be clean and presentable before you arrived, Mother,' Fen said, shooting a black look at Adam, 'but old slavedriver here kept me doing overtime.'

'On instructions, darling,' said her father. 'We wanted to be here before you got home.'

'We've already had a look round the Stables,' said Frances, cuddling Jamie. 'It's lovely. You've all worked very hard. There's hardly a thing for me to do except get pictures up and change things round a bit.'

'Told you, Fen,' said Adam, resigned.

She grinned, and took a look round the group crowded into the kitchen as usual. 'Where are the junior Savages?'

'At home for the night with my sainted parents, to cut down catering numbers,' said Jonah. 'Our young agreed only with ruinous bribes, and on condition I ordered you to Hampstead for the weekend, Fenny, so they can take you up in the Eye.'

'You mean I've got to revolve round a giant wheel in a bubble to get their company?' she said in mock terror.

'Go!' ordered Frances, and Fen took to her heels.

When she came back downstairs, she ran towards the noise coming from the drawing room, and gave a gasp of delight when Kate, with her large husband's help, heaved herself from a chair, laughing as Fen hugged her very carefully.

'It's all right, Fen, I won't break.'

'It's great to see you. You, too, Alasdair.'

Alasdair Drummond kissed her cheek, then gently lowered his wife back into her chair. 'Kate insisted on coming, so you get me, too. At this stage I go where she goes.'

'I don't suppose Jess and Lorenzo are lurking in the broom cupboard by any chance?' said Fen, flippant to hide emotion.

'No, darling,' said her mother. 'They wanted to be here, but Marco's got some virus, so Jess sent her love, and said they're looking forward to seeing you soon for your holiday.'

'If I can spare her,' said Adam, and detached his smaller son from his grandmother. 'Come on, you two, bath time.'

There was such noisy protest over this that Frances suggested the youngest Dysarts came back down for a treat. 'Put them to bed when they get tired.'

Gabriel smiled. 'OK, Grandma. Just this once.'

It was a noisy, lively evening, and by the time pudding and cheese arrived Jamie was fast asleep on his grandmother's shoulder and Hal needed only a little persuasion to accompany his brother to bed.

With showtime fast approaching Fen had found it hard to eat, but she'd done as much justice as she could to the meal, and insisted on helping clear away afterwards, putting off the moment even longer by staying to chat to Mrs Briggs while she made coffee.

'Want a hand, Fenny?' said Jonah, coming into the kitchen.

'It's ready. You take the tray; I'll bring the rest,' she said, trying to smile.

'Chin up, princess,' he said, as he followed behind. 'We're all here, rooting for you.'

Once Adam and Gabriel had rejoined them, with baby listener at the ready, Fen refilled coffee cups, then sat on the leather fender, wondering whether to wait until she was alone with her parents before dropping her bombshell or to come out with it now and get it over with.

'Frances, Tom,' said Gabriel, pre-empting her. 'I've got a confession to make. I'm afraid I did something terrible while you were away. I only hope you'll forgive me for it.' She told how she'd let slip the truth about Fenny's birth, but Fen interrupted her immediately, looking at her stricken parents in desperate appeal.

'I was the one who did something terrible, not Gabriel. I know you don't like scenes, Kate, so please don't get upset, but I just have to do this.' She launched into her story, sparing herself nothing.

With only the occasional exclamation Frances and Tom Dysart heard her out with restraint Fen was grateful for, but when she saw tears in her mother's eyes she stumbled across the room into her parents' outstretched arms.

'Don't reproach yourself,' Tom Dysart told Gabriel, who was as tearful as Fen by this time, with Leonie and Kate little better. 'It's our fault entirely. We should have told Fenny the truth years ago.'

Frances nodded, and wiped her eyes with one hand, the other stroking the glossy dark head buried against her shoulder. 'We named her Fenella, as Rachel wanted, but otherwise she was as much ours as the others from the first.'

Fen looked up at her mother in surprise. 'Rachel chose my name?'

'Yes, darling.' Frances gave her a tissue. 'Blow your nose.'

'Mind you, Fen,' said Alasdair, smiling to lighten the atmosphere. 'I wish I'd seen you perched on a piano singing torch songs.'

'Me too,' said Kate with relish.

Adam grinned as his mother shuddered. 'Actually, she wasn't half bad. If it had been someone else's sister I would have joined in the ovation.'

'Applause, not ovation, and I sat on the piano so I could sneak a look at the lyrics now and then,' said Fen, and slid to sit cross-legged at her parents' feet. 'I was petrified. I only did it as a favour to your pal Tim.'

Leonie Savage leaned forward to catch Fen's eye. 'Don't think you're the only one to run away, Fenny. I did once, too. Broke my engagement to Jonah and went back to Italy to work without a word of explanation.'

'All because she did some eavesdropping and jumped to the conclusion that *I* was your dad,' said Jonah, smiling as Fen stared at him incredulously.

'Come to think of it, though, Jonah,' said Tom, looking from one face to the other, 'it's no wonder

Leo got the wrong end of the stick. There's a marked likeness. Especially about the eyes.'

Jonah nodded. 'I look a lot like my uncle. And if you think about it Fenny and my son and heir could be brother and sister.'

'I've never seen it myself,' said Frances firmly. 'I think Fenny resembles Kate.'

'I hope our baby will, too,' said Alasdair, patting his wife's bulge.

'I'd like him to resemble *one* of us,' said Kate, smiling up at him.

'Do you know it's a boy?' asked Fen, diverted.

'Not officially. But it's a fifty-fifty chance.'

'Farthing Street!' exclaimed Tom Dysart suddenly, and leaned down towards Fen. 'That road down by the canal? I thought those houses were condemned years ago.'

'They should have been,' said Adam grimly.

'The house wasn't that bad,' protested Fen.

'It was a dump!'

'Cheap, though.' Fen looked up at her parents, determined to get everything over with in one fell swoop. 'There's something else.'

Frances braced herself. 'Out with it.'

'Even though it was a horrible little house, I found I rather liked living on my own.'

Tom nodded, and smiled at his wife. 'We've been expecting this for some time.'

'Have you?' said Fen relieved. 'You don't mind, then?'

'Where?' said Frances, resigned.

'Something trendy in Pennington centre would be nice, but I'll settle for anything reasonable I can afford.'

'Adam hasn't told you everything,' said Tom. 'On your next birthday you come into the money Rachel left you. She told us to use some of it for your education, but we've never had to do that, so it's all there, waiting.' He named a sum which took Fen's breath away. 'You could buy yourself a nice little place with that.'

'Be careful, love,' advised Kate, smiling. 'With your looks *and* money you'll have half the male population of Pennington chasing after you.'

'They won't catch me,' Fen assured her. 'I'm off men.'

'Why?' said her mother sharply.

'Working in a bar put me off some of the species.' Fen grinned. 'Present company excepted, of course.'

The party broke up early due to Kate's inability to stay awake. After kisses and goodnights had been exchanged Alasdair Drummond, who was a foot taller than his wife, with the build of the rugby forward he had once been, carried Kate out to the car for the trip to Gloucester. After waving them off Jonah left his wife to the embraces of her parents and drew Fen aside.

'My uncle was a man you'd have liked, even loved, Fenny. Try not to blame Richard, or Rachel, too much.'

'I don't any more. I went off like a rocket at first, mainly because of Aunt Helen, but I've calmed down enough to have sympathy now.'

'Good girl.' Jonah took an envelope from his pocket. 'Something I thought you might like to keep. Open it when you're alone.' He looked up as Leonie joined them. 'Ready, darling?'

'Raring to go,' she assured him.

'Are you picking Richard and the twins up on the way?' asked Fen.

'No,' said Jonah with relish. 'My sainted parents are keeping them overnight. Which is why I'm in a hurry to get my wife home to bed.'

Leo laughed and gave Fen a hug. 'Is he making you blush?'

'I'm used to him by now.'

After they'd gone it struck Fen that her parents would also be leaving shortly, to sleep in the Stables for the first time. And that maybe she ought to be going with them to the spare room there, where Rachel had slept in the past when her own parents moved over to the Stables.

'You looked tired, darling,' said Frances, eyeing

her closely. 'Why don't you pop off to bed? But don't wake the boys on your way past.'

Her mother having solved the problem for her, as usual, Fen kissed everyone goodnight and went up to the privacy of her room to open the envelope Jonah had given her. She found two photographs inside. Fen was familiar with the silver-framed study of a younger Rachel Dysart her father kept on his desk, but the informal snapshot in her hand had been taken much later, probably at the time she met Richard Savage. Tall, blonde and vital, her eyes bright with humour and intelligence, Rachel's likeness to her brother Tom was very marked, with no resemblance at all to her daughter.

Fen gazed at the photograph for some time before turning to the other one, and for a moment she thought Jonah had given her one of himself. Then she sat down with a bump as she realised that the dark, elegant man was Richard Savage, and *his* resemblance to his daughter was unmistakable. 'No wonder Rachel fell in love with you,' she told the photograph.

Next morning Fen had finished breakfast by the time Adam and Gabriel appeared.

'Good morning, folks. What's happened to the boys? It was very quiet up there when I came past.'

'Their late night knocked them out.' Adam

nodded towards the baby listener. 'They're still snoring.'

'And we had a marvellous lie-in for once,' said Gabriel thankfully. 'How are you this morning, Fenny? Did all that confessing keep you awake?'

'No. Must have been good for the soul, like they say, because I slept like a log.'

'In that case—' Adam tossed her a bunch of keys. 'Do your poor old brother a good turn and open up at Dysart's for me, would you, Fenny? I fancy a peaceful breakfast with my wife for once. I'll be along shortly.'

Fen jumped up at once. 'Will do, boss. Tell Mother and Dad I'll see them later.'

When she got to Dysart's she went straight to her little office, hung up her jacket, and stood for a minute, looking at the view of the Parade through her window. The sky was overcast, but Fen's mood was lighter than it had been for quite a while, now her parents were home and her sins both confessed and forgiven. All she had to do now was get Joe Tregenna out of her system. Somehow. She heaved a sigh, then turned with a smile as one of the younger porters arrived with the mail.

'Thanks, Colin.'

'My pleasure.' He smiled, obviously disposed to linger, and Fen, mindful of Adam's remarks, sat down at her desk and got busy, as a hint for Colin to take himself off.

The next to appear was Reg Parker, who'd started work at the auction house the same day as Tom Dysart, but so far was fiercely resisting retirement.

'Adam all right, dear?' he asked anxiously.

'Fine. He'll be in soon.'

'Good. That boy bothering you just now, was he?'

'Not in the least, Reg.'

'I'll let you get on, then.'

When Adam arrived later he was carrying a bunch of exquisite white roses.

'Gee, thanks, boss,' said Fen, startled. 'What did I do to deserve these?'

'I wondered that myself when the florist handed them over! From your ex-lover, I assume?'

Fen took the card from the small envelope and nodded. 'You want to read the card?' she added tartly, when Adam showed no signs of leaving.

'You bet.'

Fen held it out to him, and got up to find something to hold the flowers. 'I don't suppose you happen to have a Lalique vase hanging about? A chipped one would do.'

'You'll be lucky. Ask Reg for something.' He handed the card back. 'A cryptic little message. Is it Tregenna's handwriting?'

'No idea.'

'Are you going to do as he asks?'

She thought about it. 'I'm not sure,' she replied, and looked at the card again, which said curtly:

It was not. Come to the park at one.

Adam peered through the window. 'It looks like rain. Pity to let him get wet.'

'I thought you didn't like him,' said Fen, surprised.

'Only because he made you unhappy. But he's obviously trying to make amends. So if you want him, Fenny, go get him.'

She tapped the card. 'He's giving orders. I don't like that, roses or no roses.'

But she arranged the perfect blooms in the vase Reg found for her, and to Adam's amusement put them on top of a filing cabinet, where she would see them every time she looked up from her computer screen.

CHAPTER ELEVEN

FEN'S pride would keep her away from the park, and the meeting with Joe. But the scent of the roses was so distracting that when the sun came out later in the morning she gave up trying to concentrate and went in search of Adam. She found him with Reg in the disused chapel next door, discussing the new security windows. When he saw Fen beckoning he followed her outside.

'It's only half past twelve, but I'm pretty well in hand, boss, so can I have a longer lunch hour than usual?' she asked.

'To dally with your swain in the park?'

'Certainly not. I told you, I'm passing on that. I just need a run.'

'After yesterday you should be too tired for that, surely?'

'Is that a no?'

'Of course not. I'll see you later.'

Fen flew back up to her office, changed into shorts, running shoes and vest, pulled on a baseball cap, covered herself up with a raincoat and went down to her car to drive to her usual spot near the riverbank. As she shed the raincoat to start her run she smiled smugly, picturing Joe waiting in vain in the park, like a schoolboy stood up by his girlfriend. To cheer her even more it began to rain shortly before one o'clock, and on her return run to the car she got happily wet as she thought of Joe ruining one of his expensive suits.

It was almost two-thirty by the time she got back from her outrageously long lunch hour to find Adam waiting, like a caged lion, in her office.

'Where the hell have you been?' he demanded furiously. 'You're drenched.'

'Sorry I'm late, boss. But it was good to stretch my legs. So if you'll excuse me for five minutes more I'll change and tidy up—' She looked at him. 'What's the matter?'

'I was *worried*,' he thundered, surprising her.

'Why? I often do this.'

'True, but I wish you hadn't done it today. I had Tregenna in here an hour ago, soaking wet and furious, demanding to see you.'

'Really?' said Fen, startled.

'Yes, really.' Adam glowered at the memory. 'When I told him where you'd gone he gave me an earful.'

Her eyes flashed. 'It's nothing to do with him if you give me time off!'

'He meant the place where you run. Told me I should put a stop to it, make you keep to the main park.'

Fen whistled. 'I bet you liked that.'

Adam nodded grimly. 'I told him it was no damn concern of his, at which point he informed me that whether I liked it or not you were very much his concern, and took off to look for you. After he'd gone I realised he was damn right to be worried. By the time you finally turned up I was picturing assault, rape and God knows what.'

'Sorry, boss,' she said remorsefully. 'I'd better change.' She hurried off to the small cloakroom she shared with Adam. If Joe still considered her his concern, she'd better get busy with hairbrush and mascara wand in case he came back.

Adam's lips twitched when she took him some coffee by way of apology. 'Full warpaint in case Tregenna comes back with guns blazing?' he asked, amused. 'But don't you think you should ring him, Fenny? Tell him you're safe?'

She nodded, knowing Adam was right. 'I'll do it now.' She went next door to her office to ring Joe, but his cellphone number was unobtainable. With reluctance she rang Safehouse Insurance instead, where she was informed that Mr Tregenna was out, and not expected back that day.

Fen rang the flat in Chester Square as a last resort, but when Joe's recorded voice told her to leave a message she gave up, and with an irritable shrug got back to work.

To her great disappointment there was no return visit from an angry Joe Tregenna that afternoon. Neither was he lying in wait in the car park later, as Fen had hoped. But when she reached Friars Wood she cheered up at the welcome sight of her mother, hand in hand with two small grandsons, coming along the terrace to meet her.

'I'm keeping these two out of Gabriel's hair while she gets ready,' explained Frances, kissing Fen.

'You've actually managed to persuade her to go out, then? Adam told me you were going to try.'

'In the end she agreed that three babysitters might just cope. Yes, Hal,' she said, in response to her grandson's plea. 'You can play ball with Fenny for ten minutes while Grandma gets your supper ready.'

Later Fen tried to contact Joe again, but with the same result. He was probably out to dinner and his cellphone needed charging, she assured herself. And kept on worrying.

'You're restless tonight, darling,' said Tom, after Adam had managed to get Gabriel out of the house. 'Adam cracking the whip too much?'

'No, indeed. He even gave me extra time at lunch to go for a run. Mother won't let me help with dinner, so I'll catch up on the news with you.'

Fen smiled at him and curled up on the sofa, but nothing she heard took her mind off Joe until an item the end of the regional news brought her bolt upright in horror.

'A man was attacked, robbed, and left unconscious by the river in Pennington earlier today,' said the newsreader. 'The victim was expensively dressed, dark-haired and in his thirties. The police are asking anyone who might have information to contact them on—'

'Fenny?' said Tom Dysart, as she leapt to her feet. 'What's up?'

'That's where I went for my run today.'

'Did you, by God?' said her father, and got up to take her by the shoulders. 'No more of that in future, my girl. Find somewhere safer—or, better still, I'll buy you a treadmill.'

'Never mind that now, Dad,' said Fen, in an agony of impatience. 'I need to ring the police.'

After a wait to get through, and a conversation with the man in charge of the case, Fen burst into the study.

'Dad, I told the police I might know the victim. They want me to drive into the General to identify him.'

'Who is it?'

'Someone I met recently. You don't know him.'

'I'll come with you,' said Tom promptly, getting to his feet.

'No need, Dad. Mother will have a fit if we both take off without dinner.'

'I can't let you do something like that on your own, child!'

Fen smiled at him. 'Of course you can. It's just a drive to the hospital and back. Besides, it may not be the man I know. Or the poor bloke may have recovered consciousness by the time I get there and given them his name. But I have to go.'

Tom sighed. 'All right, Fenny. Let's break the news to your mother.'

Five minutes later Fen was on her way to Pennington, leaving Tom trying hard to convince his incensed wife that she should be proud of their daughter for behaving like a responsible citizen.

When Fen got to Pennington General a police constable took her to a curtained-off bed in the A&E department.

'He's still out for the count, miss, and I should warn you that he doesn't look very pretty.'

Fen took a steadying breath, then went through the curtains the constable held back for her. The man in the bed was deathly pale, his bruised, battered face half obscured by stitches and dressings. But she could have kissed him, wounds and all. Because he wasn't Joe Tregenna.

She turned to the policeman, shaking her head. 'It's not my friend. I've never seen this man before. How's he doing?'

'Badly concussed. He mutters now and then, but so far nothing coherent. He was robbed of any personal belongings, so until he comes round, or someone misses him, we're in the dark.'

They left the wounded man to the attentions of a nurse, then sat outside while the constable took notes about Fen's run, and details of any passersby she'd noticed. When she finally left the hospital she rang Friars Wood, told her father she'd be home later, then drove straight to Chester Square and heaved a sigh of relief at the sight of Joe's car. She found a place to park, then ran along the terrace of beautiful houses to ring the bell on the familiar side door.

'It's Fen,' she said when Joe's voice came through the speaker. 'Can I come up?'

There was silence for a moment, then she heard the door release and went in, her heart thumping at the sight of him, standing tall and hostile, at the head of the stairs.

'This is a delightful surprise,' he said with sarcasm. 'You were just passing?'

'No.' Fen decided against a smile as she reached the landing. 'I had to come back to Pennington tonight, so I thought I'd call to thank you for the flowers.'

'I see. Do sit down,' he added, ushering her into the main room. 'Or are you in a hurry?'

'No.'

'Then may I offer you a drink?' he asked, so formal Fen could have hit him.

'Thank you. Coffee, perhaps?'

Dauntingly forbidding in black jeans and sweater, Joe gave a curt nod and went from the room.

Fen hadn't expected him to welcome her with open arms. After his wait in the rain, followed by an abortive hunt for her afterwards, she'd been fully prepared for anger, or even orders to get lost. But Joe's cold indifference was unexpected, and a whole lot harder to bear.

When Joe returned with a steaming beaker, he maintained his cold silence as he put it down on the table beside her.

'Thank you,' she said quietly, as he sat opposite. 'Adam said you came to Dysart's today,' she said, taking the bull by the horns.

'Yes. After a wait in the rain I lost my temper, so I went round to Dysart's to ask why you hadn't had the courtesy to ring me and put me off.' He gave her a searing look. 'I suppose it amused you to think of me getting drenched.'

'It did, rather,' she admitted, and sipped some coffee, then flushed when her empty stomach responded predictably to the heat and strength of it. 'Sorry,' she muttered, embarrassed.

'Haven't you eaten?' he asked, displaying so little interest in her reply Fen didn't bother to make one. 'So,' he went on, 'I take it you're back in the bosom of your family?'

'Yes. When my parents got home I apologised humbly for behaving like a spoilt brat when Gabriel spilled the beans. But because I'm *their* spoilt brat, and they love me, they forgave me everything. Well, almost everything.' Fen smiled crookedly. 'Mother wasn't too thrilled about my cabaret act.'

He shot her a look. 'Did you mention me?'

'No.'

'Why not?'

Fen drained the coffee mug and set it back on the tray. 'You walked out on me, remember, so I didn't bother to mention our little fling.'

Joe's mouth tightened. 'Is that how you think of it?'

'I don't think about it at all,' she lied. 'Thank you for the coffee. I must go.'

He shook his head. 'Not before I know why you came. If it was just to thank me for the flowers a polite phone call, even a note, would have done.'

And would have been a lot better than sitting here with a pair of cold blue eyes freezing her to the marrow. 'I did ring you. But your mobile was off.'

'You could have rung me here.'

'I did, but you weren't in.'

'You could have left a message.'

'I wish I had now,' she assured him, and glanced at her watch. 'It's late—'

'It's not even nine yet,' Joe pointed out. 'Or are you meeting someone?'

'Like this? No.'

His eyes moved over her jeans and baggy sweater to the hair escaping from the ribbon failing to hold it back from her scrubbed face. 'So what exactly *are* you doing in Pennington at this time of night?'

'I had to go to the hospital.'

'What?' Joe's indifference fell away like a cloak. 'Why? Were you hurt? What happened? I went looking everywhere for you this afternoon—'

'How were you dressed?'

'What the hell does that matter?'

'On the news tonight I heard that a man had been attacked and robbed on the riverbank this afternoon, and left unconscious. The description fitted you, so I rang the police and they asked me to drive to the General to identify the victim.'

He stared at her incredulously. 'On your own?'

'Yes.' Fen shrugged. 'As I told my loudly protesting parents, I'm a big girl now.'

Joe leaned forward, hands linked between his knees, his eyes urgent now. 'Have you any idea how worried I was when I couldn't find you this afternoon? I got soaked to the skin, dropped my bloody phone in a puddle, and had to find a pay-phone before I could ring Dysart's to see if you were back. When I heard you were safe and sound in your office, I was so furious I could have wrung your neck, so instead of charging up to your office to do just that I went home.'

Fen decided against grovelling. 'Why didn't you pick up when I rang here?'

'I was at the pool, working off my mood.' He shrugged. 'I swim; you run.' His eyes darkened. 'But for God's sake, Fen, find a safer place than the towpath. You say this man got mugged today. Have you thought what could have happened to you?'

'I have since. Adam read the Riot Act when I got back to work, and Dad was muttering darkly about a treadmill as I left home tonight.'

'I don't blame him.' Joe gave her a curious look. 'Are you glad to be living at home again?'

'Yes and no,' she said, with a sigh. 'Don't get me wrong. It's great to have my parents back and my confession over with, but now they've finally moved into the Stables I feel I don't belong anywhere.'

'Isn't there room for you there?'

'Oh, yes. A newly decorated spare room I could move into right this minute. And I still have my own room in the main house. One of the few with its own bathroom, I might add. No one in the world is less homeless than Fenella Dysart.' She smiled. 'But, gross though it was, Farthing Street taught me that I really like living on my own.'

'How do your parents feel about that?'

'Resigned on my mother's part, but Dad's been expecting it for some time. He has three other daughters, remember, and they all did the same in turn. It's different for Adam. Friars Wood is his inheritance.'

'So where do you intend to live?'

'A flat in the city centre would be nice, but that might be expensive—' She paused. 'Though that's not such a problem now.'

'Why?'

She smiled brightly. 'I've just discovered I'm an heiress! Or I will be on my next birthday. Rachel left me a lot of money.'

Joe's eyes turned cold again. 'So you're not even a poor little rich girl now, just rich.'

'It's not a fortune. But enough to buy a reasonable flat.' She glanced at her watch. 'I really must go.'

Joe got to his feet. 'Come and look at the Patrick Heron print first—don't worry,' he added, 'it's not up in my bedroom.'

'A pity to keep it where no one sees it,' she agreed calmly, though it occurred to her that for all she knew there could have been a succession of women in Joe's bedroom since she was there last. Hating the very thought of it, she moved to the other half of the room to look at the vivid colours and shapes in the abstract screen-print. 'Amazing! It should look out of place in a room of this period, but actually it's perfect there.'

'There hasn't been anyone,' Joe said abruptly.

Cursing his talent for reading her mind, Fen smiled at him. 'Bad luck.'

'I meant what I said.'

'Your private life is your own business, Joe.'

'I'm talking about the message I sent with the roses.'

'Ordering me to the park?' she said sweetly, turning to go. But Joe barred her way.

'There was something before that.'

'I know. Very cryptic.'

Joe moved nearer. 'It was in answer to your parting shot last Friday. About basic sex. As I said on the card, it was not. At least it wasn't for me. Would I have gone tearing off to look for you this afternoon if I didn't care about you?'

'How do I know?' she snapped. 'Not so long ago you made it very plain I don't merit the Tregenna seal of approval.'

'If you mean that night in Farthing Street—'

'That's the one. The night you eavesdropped and found there was more to me than you knew.'

He shrugged. 'I suspected that all along.'

'Unlike gullible little me. I believed *you*

implicitly.' Fen turned away abruptly. 'I shouldn't have come here—'

'Wait.' Joe caught her hand. 'I've got a proposition to make. Not that kind of proposition,' he added as she glared at him. 'Come and sit down again.'

Fen allowed herself to be led back to the sofa, and this time Joe sat beside her, holding on to the hand she tried to pull away.

'I know I hurt you that night. But I was mad as hell at the time. I wanted to hit out at you in any way I could, and came up with the brilliant idea of luring you back for a second interview so I could strut my stuff as the head honcho.' His mouth twisted. 'I told myself you wouldn't come, but I paid the earth for a new suit that weekend just the same, purely to impress you if you did turn up.'

'I didn't notice it,' said Fen, astonished. 'All I could see was the triumph on your face as you watched me walk across miles of carpet.'

'You liked my office, then,' he said, smoothing her hand.

Fen promptly removed it from his grasp. 'How you must have enjoyed gloating over me.'

'I did,' he admitted frankly. 'Until you got up to leave. Then it struck me that once you were out through that door I might never see you again. I told myself it was a good thing, that we weren't suited—you were too young for me, and—'

'A spoilt brat!'

'I've had time to regret that.' Joe turned her towards him. 'I've missed you, Fen.'

Good, she thought exultantly. 'You said something about a proposition,' she reminded him.

'So I did.' His eyes softened. 'I enjoyed our lunch in the park. Did you?'

'Very much. I adore crab sandwiches.'

'I *meant*,' he growled, 'that it was good just to be with you, simply to walk and talk with you. I intended to make that clear afterwards, but you cut the ground from under my feet with your parting shot about sex.'

She shrugged. 'You asked me to go home with you, so what did you expect?'

'Whatever it was, I didn't get it! I took off to stay with my brother in London for the weekend instead, to take my mind off you. It didn't work.' Joe's smile set her heart pounding. 'So I've thought of a way to convince you that it's not just sex between us. In other words, Miss Dysart, I intend to come courting.'

CHAPTER TWELVE

'AN OLD-FASHIONED phrase,' said Fen, when she'd recovered the power of speech. 'Are you sure you mean courting?'

'Yes.' He moved nearer. 'I admit that if I gave in to my baser instincts I'd pick you up right now and carry you off to my bedroom—'

'The one no other female has set foot in?' she retorted, her voice tart to hide the heat his words ignited.

'I wasn't quite truthful about that—' He grabbed her as she flung away. 'I mean that I've found a wonderful lady who cleans for me twice a week— including the bedroom.'

Fen glowered at him and thrust his hands away. 'Doing a little cage-rattling yourself, Joe?'

'Did it work?'

'No.'

'Liar!' Joe grinned, looking so different from the cold, hostile man of earlier on Fen couldn't help smiling in response.

'OK,' she said casually. 'Come courting if you want. Sounds rather fun.'

'Fun!' He shook his head in disbelief. 'I ply you with expensive roses, get soaked to the skin waiting for you, go mad with worry after chasing along the river looking for you, and you think it's fun—?' He broke off as her phone rang.

Fen took it from her bag, unsurprised to hear her mother's voice.

'I'm fine, Mother, and I'm just about to drive home. See you soon.'

She put the phone back, eyeing Joe wryly. 'Are you sure about this? I've got a big family. And they'll all ask awkward questions if you come calling. I don't take boyfriends home to Friars Wood.'

'I'm not one of your boyfriends,' said Joe emphatically, and turned her face up to his. 'I'm your lover, Fenny. And don't flash those eyes at me. I know only your nearest and dearest call you that.' He pulled her into his arms. 'But at the moment I am the nearest. And if I'm not the dearest yet, I damn well intend to be.' His mouth closed over hers in a kiss meant to convince, and Fen kissed him back. Then, overwhelmed by reaction to the various stresses of the evening, she hugged him hard.

'I'm so glad it wasn't you,' she muttered into his sweater.

Joe tipped her face up. 'And if you were afraid I was at death's door, and anxious enough to go haring off to the hospital to find out, it's useless to pretend you don't care about me.'

'Then I won't bother.' Fen drew in a deep, unsteady breath. 'When I saw that poor man lying there, battered and bruised and out to the world, I could have kissed him. Because he wasn't you.'

'Kiss me instead,' ordered Joe huskily, and Fen, happy to obey this time, kissed him with such wanton lack of inhibition he soon pushed her away. 'Any more of that,' he said, the laughter back in his eyes, 'and I'll think you just want me for sex.'

'Certainly not,' she said primly. 'At least, not on the first date.'

Joe grinned and smoothed her hair back. 'But this isn't our first date.'

'If you meant what you said about courting, maybe we should think of it that way, Joe.'

He nodded slowly. 'You're right. We'll look on this as square one, go on from there, and do our damnedest not to get back to it this time.'

'At least you know everything about me now,' Fen assured him. 'What you see is what you get, warts and all.'

'Warts?' said Joe in mock horror. 'Where?'

'You don't get to see those on a first date either!'

* * *

When Fen got home, tired, hungry, but blissfully happy, four pairs of eyes turned on her in relief when she put her head round the study door.

'I'm home.'

'About time, too,' said Frances, jumping up. 'Have you eaten?'

'No. But don't worry, I'll make a sandwich or something.'

'You will not, Fenella Dysart. I'll heat up your dinner and bring it in on a tray. *Was* it your friend at the hospital?'

'No,' said Fen thankfully. 'It was a complete stranger, poor man.'

The moment Frances was out of the room Adam pounced on Fen. 'You thought it was Tregenna?'

Fen nodded. 'The man's description fitted Joe perfectly. And because he never came back from searching for me I jumped to the obvious conclusion.'

'Come and sit here,' said Gabriel with sympathy, patting the place beside her.

'Who,' said Tom Dysart, fixing his daughter with a steely look, 'is this Tregenna?'

'A man I met while you were away.'

'It's all right, Dad, put the shotgun away,' teased Adam. 'I've met him, too. Tregenna's single, solvent, several years older than Fenny, and, in her eyes at least, quite present-able.'

'And she cares enough for him to go rushing off

to the hospital,' said Tom thoughtfully. 'Does he reciprocate, Fenny?'

'You'd certainly think so if you'd seen him today at Dysart's,' said Adam. 'He blasted off at me for not taking proper care of my sister, then went charging off to look for her in the rain.'

'A real knight errant,' said Gabriel, impressed.

'As it happens, that's how we met—' Fen broke off as she heard her mother returning. 'Tell you later,' she whispered.

'Fortunately,' said Frances severely, as she set a tray on Fen's knees, 'I'd made an extra large cassoulet so Gabriel and Adam could have some for dinner tomorrow night.'

'Wonderful,' said Fen, and tucked into her steaming bowlful while she described her visit to the battered stranger at the General. 'The policeman told me his shoes and clothes were expensive, but no name-tags.'

'But why was a man like that on the riverbank in the pouring rain?' said Gabriel.

Avoiding his mother's eye, Adam informed his wife that it was a popular place for a certain kind of assignation. 'Lots of cover,' he added vaguely.

'Anyway, Mother, the description fitted someone I've met recently,' said Fen, wiping bread round her bowl. 'His name's Joe Tregenna, and because I like him rather a lot I went dashing off to the hospital to see if he was the victim. But fortunately—for Joe, at least—it wasn't.'

'But surely you haven't been at the hospital all this time?' asked Frances.

'No. I went round to see Joe before coming home.' Fen shrugged. 'I tried ringing him earlier but he wasn't in. And after seeing that poor man in such a state in the A&E I wanted to make sure Joe was all right.'

'Why shouldn't he have been?' said Tom, smiling.

'I don't know. I just needed to see him.'

Frances looked narrowly at her daughter. 'You say you like this man a lot. What does that mean, exactly?'

'I'm not sure yet,' said Fen, though she was. 'Let's just say Joe and I are going out together.' Because for the time that was wiser than staying in together. Whatever Joe meant by courting, her own idea of it was old-fashioned dating.

After Frances and Tom had gone off to the Stables, something Fen still found strange, Gabriel asked Adam to make tea. 'Or a nightcap for you, or whatever,' she told him. 'Because I'm not going to bed until Fen tells all.'

Adam grinned as the phone rang in Fen's bag.

'Fenny?' said Joe. 'You didn't ring me.'

'Was I supposed to?'

'Yes. Rules of engagement. You drive home alone; you ring me when you get there. Right?'

'Right.'

'You're not alone?'

'Right.'

'Shall I ring again in half an hour?'

'Right.'

Fen put the phone away and fluttered her eyelashes at Adam. 'Yes, it was Joe, and, yes, I'd love some tea.'

'Coming up. But don't start without me.'

'I'd better do the tea,' said Gabriel. 'You check on the boys, darling—don't go to sleep, Fenny.'

Fen stretched out on the sofa with a sigh of deep, unadulterated joy, sleep the last thing on her mind as she went over every detail of the evening. And in record time Gabriel was back with two mugs of tea, Adam following behind with his single malt.

'So come on,' he said. 'How *did* you meet Tregenna?'

Fen described the attempted mugging in Farthing Street, and Joe's dash to the rescue. 'Though they were only kids—so I could have sorted them myself without his help, really.'

Adam groaned. 'Don't say a word to Mother, for God's sake, or she'll never cope with the idea of your living alone.'

'Are you going to?' said Gabriel.

'Definitely. It's more than time I did.'

'I meant that maybe Mr Tregenna has other ideas.'

'We're just good friends,' said Fen demurely, then drank her tea down and kissed them both goodnight. 'See you in the morning—I hope Jamie keeps to his own bed tonight.'

'Amen,' said Adam fervently.

Fen's phone rang the moment she closed her bedroom door behind her.

'Are you in bed yet?' asked Joe.

'Not quite. But I'm alone in my room.'

'Good. I just wanted to say goodnight properly.' And for several minutes he did just that, leaving Fen in a happy daze afterwards as she drifted into sleep.

Fen spent most of the morning in the chapel with Adam next day, making notes on the lots for general auction. When Joe rang mid-morning Adam grinned and took himself out of earshot.

'Will you do me the honour of having lunch with me, Miss Dysart?' said Joe.

'Let me see,' she said, pretending to consult her diary. 'I have a window between one and two.'

'Good. So do I.'

This marked the beginning of a new stage in their relationship, something Fen looked on more as a pattern than a routine. It was exciting not to know in advance when Joe would ring to ask her out to lunch, or say he had tickets for the theatre, or had booked a meal somewhere. But, making it clear he meant to keep his word, Joe never suggested a meal at his flat. And Fen felt the need to wait a while before she asked Joe to Friars Wood.

In her spare time she haunted estate agents in an effort to find a flat. Her mother had become resigned to the inevitable about Fen's home of her own, but remained adamant on the subject of finding something in a secure apartment building with a concierge.

'Which makes life difficult, because they're few and far between,' Fen told Joe one night, over dinner in a small Italian restaurant.

'The tenants below me are moving out,' said Joe. 'Now you're an heiress you could buy that.'

She shook her head regretfully. 'Above my touch. I just want somewhere pleasant and secure, and reasonable enough to give me money over to furnish it and still have a nest-egg left. But nothing's turned up yet.'

'Rent something while you search,' said Joe, filling her wine glass.

Fen gazed at him, impressed. 'What a brilliant idea! I should have thought of it before. It would save all this mileage I'm totting up.'

'And I could see you to your door instead of watching you drive away from me every night,' he pointed out, and smiled. 'I trust you've noticed how exemplary my behaviour has been lately? One goodnight kiss and I send you home to bed instead of taking you home to mine.'

'I'm glad to hear you still want to do that,' she assured him, 'but I like this courting idea.'

'I like the *idea* of it myself,' he agreed, and sighed heavily. 'But in practice it's hellish frustrating. You look so delicious in that dress—'

'You could eat me for dessert?' she said demurely.

'You're enjoying this,' he accused.

'You bet. If this is courting I love it.' She sobered. 'Not that I wouldn't enjoy an evening with you on your sofa just as much, watching television or just talking. But—'

'You don't trust me not to hustle you off to bed?' he said morosely.

'It's more a case of not trusting myself, Joe.' She met his eyes squarely. 'After we broke up I missed you in every way, including the bed part. Which was an eye-opener. I didn't know that would happen.'

Joe's eyes gleamed dark in the candlelight as he leaned towards her. 'That you could want someone physically in their absence?'

She nodded. 'I suppose you think I'm pretty naive?'

'Not at all. It's very ego-inflating as far as I'm concerned, Miss Dysart.' He reached out a hand to take hers. 'Let's go.'

Fen soon realised why Joe was in such a hurry to leave. Instead of taking her to Dysart's car park he drove a short way out of town and parked beside the river in the starlit darkness. He unfastened his seatbelt, then leaned to release hers and drew her into his arms.

'I need more than one kiss tonight, Fenny,' he whispered, and kissed her with such hunger she responded in kind. The kisses grew wild, their caressing hands even more so, and at last Joe groaned like a man in pain as he raised his head.

'You're killing me. How long must I keep up the courting?' he whispered against her flushed cheek.

Fen drew back to look at him. 'I don't know. I suppose it rather depends on what you have in mind once you think I've been courted enough. Certain things remain unchanged, Joe Tregenna. I'm still a lot younger than you, still looked on at home as the baby of the family. Which accounts for the famous spoilt brat syndrome.'

Joe stroked a hand down her cheek. 'Let's forget that. Preferably for ever. And I don't care a toss about your age any more. If you've got any growing up to do you can do it with me. Forget about finding a flat, Fenny. Share mine.'

'Come live with you and be your love?' she said breathlessly.

Joe's eyes darkened. 'You're my love whether

you live with me or not, Fenny. But I want you with me on a permanent basis. I'll even start running with you instead of swimming—anything to avoid a repeat of that day I couldn't find you.'

'Greater love hath no man,' she said, purposely flippant.

'Exactly,' he agreed, not flippant at all, and pulled her close to kiss her.

'How do you feel,' said Fen, taking the plunge, 'about coming to lunch at Friars Wood next Sunday?'

Joe drew back in surprise. 'After the way I tore into Adam last time we met, is that a good idea?'

'Of course it is. Dysarts are a hospitable lot, and my parents have been keen to make your acquaintance from the moment I said we were going out together.' She laughed softly. 'Sorry for the schoolgirl-speak. I couldn't say we were lovers.'

'We aren't actually lovers at the moment,' he pointed out. 'But if meeting your family is a step towards getting us that way again I'm very happy to come on Sunday. How many Dysarts on the reception committee?'

'Mother, Dad, Gabriel, Adam, and Hal and Jamie. If all goes well you can meet a few more later.'

'I'll take you to Polruan before that,' he said, surprising her.

Fen's eyes widened. 'You want me to meet your family?'

'Why the surprise? Fair's fair. I run the Dysart gauntlet first, then you come and convince my mother you're good enough for me.'

'How will I do that?' she said, alarmed.

Joe kissed her nose. 'Just be yourself—it works for me.'

When she got home Fen went straight to the Stables to make an immediate request to bring a visitor to Sunday lunch. Her parents received this with enthusiasm, candid about their curiosity to meet Joe Tregenna. In the past young men had called to take Fen out, brought her home from parties, given her lifts to college and jammed the telephone lines with their calls. But she had never asked to bring one home for a family meal.

'If we ask Kate and Alasdair there won't be enough room here,' said Frances immediately, her mind already on catering. 'I'll ask Gabriel if I can do lunch over there.'

Tom winked at Fen. 'Your mother still hasn't got to grips with the new cooker here.'

'Nonsense! Though I do prefer the old one,' Frances admitted. 'Tell Gabriel I'll be over in the morning to ask her myself.'

'She's hardly likely to say no,' said Fen, laughing. 'But you don't have to invite the whole gang, Mother.'

'Try convincing her of that,' said her father, resigned. 'At least you gave her a couple of days' notice. I suppose I can look forward to a long session in the supermarket tomorrow.'

Fen chuckled and kissed them goodnight, then went over to the main house to break the news to Gabriel. 'Sorry to land you with all this, folks.'

'No problem,' said Adam. 'My wife will be delighted to hand the Sunday roast over to Mother.'

'Absolutely,' said Gabriel, eyes sparkling. 'Shall I get Mrs Briggs up to look after the boys?'

'No need. I want the boys part of the scene. I'm sure Joe'll keep them amused for you.'

'Does this mean things have taken a serious turn, Fenny?' said Adam.

'Yes. He's even taking me to Cornwall.'

'A little holiday to celebrate whatever it is you're celebrating?' said Gabriel.

'No,' said Fen, pulling a face, 'to meet his mother.'

'Serious stuff, then!'

'Possibly. So I'd better report in to Joe with the official invitation.'

Frances Dysart soon found her list of Dysarts shorter than she would have liked. Leonie, Jonah and their children were in Tuscany with Jess, and Kate refused with regret because she was forbidden any journey longer than a mile or two until the birth.

'How about bringing this man of yours here to tea soon instead, Fenny?' suggested Kate to Fen. 'I'd love to meet him.'

Frances and Tom Dysart spent next morning in Pennington, stocking up on supplies for the forthcoming lunch party, then went to the auction house so Tom could spend a happy hour there watching while thief-proof bars were being installed on the windows in the chapel annexe. But at last Frances sent Fen to tell him it was lunchtime, and invited Adam to join them.

'Sorry, Mother, I'm due in Tetbury shortly. But you can take Fen. She's meeting Tregenna tonight, so she can cancel their picnic in the park and make him wait until later for the pleasure of her company.'

'He's busy today, anyway,' said Fen, and grinned at her parents. 'But in preference to lunch with my mummy and daddy I would have cancelled—honest.'

'If you say so,' said Tom, laughing.

'Do you spend your lunch hour with him every day, then?' said Frances.

'When we're both free at the same time, yes,' said Fen. 'But Joe often has meetings and so on, or has a business lunch. And sometimes he takes a turn at the phones.'

'But I thought you said he was a founder of this insurance company?' said her father, surprised.

'He is, in partnership with his two brothers at the London office. But Joe likes to stay involved in the day-to-day business of the firm, and he spends a few hours a week listening in and taking calls from customers, right alongside his foot soldiers.'

'I'm impressed,' said Frances.

'I'll tell Joe that later. He's picking me up here when he finishes.' Fen smiled at Adam. 'So you can go straight home to your wife from Tetbury, and I'll lock up myself.'

During the afternoon Joe rang Fen to say he'd be a bit later than expected, but would come for her as soon as he could get away.

Once the more valuable pieces were transferred to the Dysart safety repository for the weekend, and both buildings were checked and secure, with burglar alarms set, Fen saw the staff off, then took an overnight bag from the boot of her car and went up through the silent building to her office, to begin making herself as good to look at as she could for Joe.

Her suit exchanged for the scarlet top and white jeans once worn on a less happy occasion, Fen made herself some coffee while she waited for Joe, and sat down at her desk with a book.

Absorbed in the plot, Fen was slow to realise that something was wrong. She put the book down at last and sat very still, listening. The old building was full of creaks and groans, as usual, but she was used to that. And due to the complex alarm system Adam had updated during his new security drive she had no fear of intruders.

Fen collected her phone, then left her little office and went on a tour, making a painstaking inspection of every nook and cranny on every floor of the premises. She still couldn't pinpoint any cause for alarm. Yet some sixth sense was still warning her that something wasn't right. She locked up, and went next door to the chapel annexe that housed the less choice items, thankful that there were far fewer of them than usual, due to the most recent auction. But the moment she was through the door Fen stiffened in sudden dread as she slammed it shut behind her. Smoke. She could smell *smoke*!

She rushed to check the various lots, and was flying up the steep stairs to the upper gallery when all the smoke alarms went off at once. Fen rang the fire brigade, then forced herself to search methodically through the packing cases for the point of origin. She gasped in horror when she saw a tongue of flame in the smoke billowing from a wooden crate filled with straw. She yanked one of the fire extinguishers from the wall and trained it on the flames licking from the crate at frightening speed. Coughing, she ran for another extinguisher, almost hysterical with relief when she heard the sound of approaching fire engines.

The fire chief led her outside while his team of firefighters put out the fire and made an intensive check to see that nothing was smouldering elsewhere in the building. Fen was given some oxygen as a precaution, then the young firefighter bending over her was thrust bodily aside and Joe, face ashen and eyes blazing with shock, snatched her into his arms.

'Watch it, sir, she needs air,' warned the firefighter.

'My God, darling, are you hurt?' demanded Joe, ignoring him. 'What in hell happened?'

'I'm not quite sure. But good old feminine intuition put me on the alert,' she said hoarsely, and leaned against him gratefully as she coughed again. 'Or maybe I'm psychic. I just had a sudden feeling something was wrong, so I searched everywhere next door first, then came in here and found a crate about to burst into flames.'

'Why the devil didn't you ring me? I'd have dropped everything and run, woman!'

'I didn't have time once I saw the flames.' Fen looked down at herself in disgust. 'Ugh! Just look at me. I'm filthy.'

'But safe and sound, Miss Dysart,' said the fire chief. 'My watch will carry on a while longer, until they're satisfied. I see you've been having some work done.'

She nodded. 'Security bars for the chapel windows. The men are coming back on Monday to finish up.'

Joe shot her a glance. 'They've been working today?'

'Yes. They were welding most of this afternoon, but left about five.'

'That's the cause, then,' said the fire chief decisively. 'Probably a minute spark of hot metal got into the crate without anyone noticing, and took a while to ignite. Lucky you were on hand, Miss Dysart, or a lot of damage could have been done before we got here.'

'I'd better ring Adam and my father. Though how to do that without sending Mother into orbit I don't quite know,' said Fen, and began coughing again at the very thought.

'Give me the numbers and I'll ring,' ordered Joe. 'And the moment one of them gets here, Fenny, I'm taking you to the hospital for a check-up.'

While Joe was on the phone the fire chief checked with the men of his watch as they came out of the chapel, then smiled at her in reassurance. 'All safe, Miss Dysart. Best to lock up here and sit quietly in your office until Adam comes.'

Once the fire engines had left Joe secured the chapel for Fen, unlocked the door into the main auction house, then half carried her upstairs when sudden reaction hit her in the knees.

'Do you have any brandy?' he demanded, as he lowered her gently into her chair.

'No,' she gasped. 'I hate the stuff. I just want water. And a lot of cuddling.'

'Drink first, then as much cuddling as you like,' he promised her unsteadily, and fetched a glass of water from the cloakroom.

Joe stood over Fen as she drank thirstily, then held out his hand. 'I seem to remember from my previous visit that there's a very large swivel chair behind Adam's desk. You can sit there until the others come.'

But when they got next door Joe sat in the chair himself and drew her down on his lap. Fen subsided into his arms thankfully, then immediately shot upright again.

'I'm ruining your shirt!'

Joe said something short and to the point about the shirt and pulled her back against him, smoothing his hand over her hair.

In response to the hypnotic stroking the shaking inside quietened, and Fen remembered to ask how Adam and her father had taken the news.

'Their only concern was you,' said Joe, his arms tightening. 'But that's it, Fenny. You're moving in with me right away.'

'OK,' she said drowsily.

'No arguments?'

'Later. Right now I'm too tired.'

When Adam came bursting into the office a few minutes later he stopped short in the doorway at the sight of his filthy sister asleep on Joe Tregenna's lap. 'Is she all right, Joe?'

'Shaken, but not too much stirred by her adventures.' Joe smiled down at the sleeping face with a look in his eyes that scotched any doubts Adam might have had about his feelings. 'She's quite a lady, your sister.'

Fen struggled awake, then sat up at the sight of her brother. 'I'm so *sorry*, Adam. I just couldn't find the source of the fire at first.'

Adam plucked her to her feet and held her so tightly she protested. 'As long as you're in one piece, to hell with anything else.'

It was a sentiment Tom Dysart agreed with wholeheartedly when he arrived. By that time Fen had washed some of the grime from her face, but had given up on her clothes.

'Did Mother get in a panic, Dad?'

'Oddly enough, not as much as you might think. But she wants you home, a.s.a.p.' He held out his hand to Joe. 'You must be Joe Tregenna. I'm Tom Dysart, and I can't thank you enough for being here when you were needed.'

'I wish to God I'd got here sooner,' said Joe, shaking hands. 'But Fenny was too busy firefighting to ring me. Now you're here I'm taking her to the General for a check-up.'

'I should have thought of that myself,' said Adam with remorse. 'Look, Joe, after that could you drive Fenny home to Stavely while Dad and I check on things here? She can leave her car here.'

'With pleasure,' said Joe promptly. 'Come on, darling, let's get it over with. By the way,' he added to the others, 'the fire chief thought the cause could have been a spark from the welding this afternoon.'

By the time Fen had been examined at the General, and blood tests taken as a precaution, it was almost nine before they arrived at Friars Wood.

'This is Joe Tregenna, girls,' said Fen, and smiled at Gabriel from her mother's arms. 'He came to my rescue again.'

'I'm very grateful to you, Mr Tregenna,' said Frances fervently.

'I did nothing, Mrs Dysart. Fenny had it all in hand before I even got there,' Joe assured her, taking the hand he was offered.

'This is Gabriel, Joe,' said Fen.

'How do you do, Mrs. Dysart—?'

'Call me Gabriel,' she said promptly. 'Push the dog away and come inside.'

'Yes, indeed,' said Frances, able to smile now she was sure her daughter was in one piece. 'You're a mess, and you smell of smoke, Fenny. Gabriel and I will entertain Joe in the kitchen while you scrub yourself. And throw those clothes away. I never want to see them again.'

Fen shot a look at Joe. 'Remember the last time I wore them?'

'Vividly,' he said, poker-faced. 'I never want to see them again either.'

Nobly refraining from asking why, Frances told her daughter to hurry. 'By the time Tom and Adam get here I hope to have some sort of meal ready.'

'And in the meantime I'll give Joe a drink,' said Gabriel, and smiled at Fen. 'No peeking at the boys on your way, Auntie, please.'

By the time Fen came downstairs again, in pink cotton trousers and a white T-shirt, hair damp and her face scrubbed clean, Joe's smoke-grimed shirt had been changed for one of Adam's and the three men were seated at the table already laid for supper, with a bottle of red wine breathing in readiness while Gabriel helped Frances with the meal.

'We're having a little something Mother made earlier, Fen,' said Adam, grinning.

'It was intended for Sunday, actually,' said Frances, 'but since Joe's already here we might as well eat it now. Sit down, Fenny, you look tired.'

'This is very kind of you, Mrs Dysart,' said Joe, while Tom carved a joint of hot, succulent ham.

'You were meant to have lunch in the dining room with all the trimmings on Sunday, but right now I'd rather see you fed than stand on ceremony,' Frances said briskly, 'so it's a bit basic tonight.'

'Nothing could be better than this,' Joe said with feeling. He smiled ruefully at his hostess. 'I intended to come bearing gifts on Sunday, to further my cause.'

'You furthered it a lot more by taking Fen to the hospital tonight,' Adam assured him, filling his glass.

'No more for me, thanks,' said Joe with regret. 'I'm driving.'

Frances exchanged a look with her husband. 'Why not stay here tonight, Joe? You deserve more than one glass of wine after all this excitement.'

'Good idea,' said Gabriel. 'He can sleep in Jess's room.'

Joe made a half-hearted protest, but after a smile from Fen he agreed gratefully. 'It took years off my life to see the fire brigade at Dysart's when I got there. I wasn't too thrilled to find Fenny being fussed over by a young hunk of a firefighter either,' he said, narrowing his eyes at her.

'I didn't even notice him,' she said with regret.

When Frances and Tom left for their own quarters, late that night, Gabriel went upstairs with Fen to install Joe in Jess's room and inform him that the bathroom opposite was all his. 'If you hear my sons in the night I apologise in advance.'

'After the traumas of the day, followed by that fantastic meal and Adam's wine, I doubt I'll hear a thing,' Joe assured her.

'I'll leave you to say your goodnights, then,' said Gabriel demurely. 'Sleep well.'

When the door closed behind her Fen flew into Joe's arms, her face upturned for the kiss she'd been longing for all evening. 'I'd better let you go,' he said at last, with reluctance, and Fen kissed him again, and went from the room. Five minutes later she was back—in her dressing gown. She shrugged it off as she tiptoed to the bed in the moonlight, then slid into Joe's arms.

'Is this allowed?' he whispered, holding her close.

'I doubt that Adam will come in here and throw me out.' She burrowed her face against his bare shoulder. 'But I don't care if he does. I'll have nightmares on my own tonight. I feel safe here with you, Joe. Will you just hold me in your arms until I fall asleep?'

'Tonight and every night for the rest of your life,' he said huskily.

When Joe woke next morning he was alone in the bed, but a small boy stood at the end of it, his unwavering blue eyes bright with curiosity.

'I'm Hal,' he announced.

Joe sat up, pushing his hair back. 'Hi, there. I'm Joe.'

'Are you Fenny's lover?'

'Yes, he is,' said Fen, hurrying in. She took Hal by the hand. 'I gather you two have introduced yourselves? This is my nephew, the elephant.'

'I'm not an elephant!' said Hal indignantly.

'You've got a memory like an elephant. Big ears like one, too,' she told him, and rolled her eyes at the grinning man in the bed. 'With Hal it's once heard and never forgotten.'

'Useful when you get to school,' said Joe.

'I go to school already,' said Hal loftily, then beamed. 'But not today because it's Saturday.'

'Gabriel says if you can bear the thought of breakfast *en famille*, Joe,' said Fenny, leading Hal to the door, 'she'll have it ready by the time you get down.'

'I'll have to run,' said Adam, swallowing his coffee later. 'Reg Parker's meeting me at the chapel to assess the damage. But you're excused today, Fen. Get a good rest.'

'Fat chance of that here,' said his wife, and smiled at Joe. 'Why don't you take Fen home with you for some peace and quiet?'

'How did Gabriel know I was about to suggest that?' asked Joe, on their journey back to Pennington.

'Those sleepy blue eyes of hers are very clear-sighted,' she informed him. 'She likes you. Mother and Dad like you too, fortunately. They didn't bat an eyelash when I said I'd be staying with you tonight.'

'Does "fortunately" mean you would have refused to come with me if they had?'

'No. But I prefer to receive their blessing.' She gave him a wry little smile. 'They've never given it up to now.'

Joe cast a glance at her. 'Didn't they like the previous men in your life?'

'I didn't actually live with any of them. At least, not in this way.'

'What is "this way"?'

Fen was silent for a moment. 'It's different with you,' she said slowly. 'I realise, now, that I was never in love with the others.'

'Whereas,' said Joe, putting a hand on hers, 'you and I belong together, Fenella Dysart.'

Once they were back in Chester Square they put away the food they'd bought on the way, then Joe ordered Fen to a sofa.

For once Fen was happy to obey orders, and relaxed against the cushions to watch the rain dripping through the trees in Chester Square, feeling utterly at peace with the world. Soon, she knew, this feeling of lassitude would go, and she'd want to be up and running again. But for now it was good just to be here. With Joe.

After lunch Joe took Fen by the hand and pulled her up.

'I've got something to show you.' He led her upstairs to the bedroom, and grinned at the look on her face when she saw a new television and VCR strategically placed for best viewing from the bed. 'The television in your bedroom was the sole thing I approved of in Farthing Street,' he informed her.

'So this is what you do in your spare time!'

He shook his head. 'I've made sure everything works, but I've been waiting for you before I actually watch anything. So you can get this rest they advised at the hospital, and we can watch horse-racing, athletics or cricket at the same time.'

'A lovely thought,' she said huskily, 'but I'm not an invalid.' She moved into his arms, looking up into eyes which darkened as their bodies touched. 'You know what I'd really like right now?'

Joe's arms tightened. 'Tell me, and you shall have it.'

'I long for some of that love in the afternoon I passed on recently.'

Joe's mouth was on hers before the words were out, and Fen melted against him, her hands clasped round his neck, her body instantly fluid and hot under his touch. She responded to his kisses with open-mouthed abandon, and their feverish hands grew clumsy with haste as they undressed each other, both of them vibrating with impatience until they were naked together in the bed. With the curtains drawn against the grey afternoon, one crimson-shaded lamp adding a glow of warmth to the heat they generated between them, the world contracted, leaving only the room and the bed and the murmured endearments and explosive gasps of delight as they brought each other to a state of arousal which was almost pain before Joe abandoned his control and slid inside her. Fen responded with rapture, her hands importuning on his shoulders and her heart hammering against his as they reached the ultimate annihilating pleasure before free-falling back to earth.

'If that's love in the afternoon,' said Fen after a long interval of recovery, 'I like it.'

'Beats cricket,' agreed Joe, then turned on his back and drew her close against him. 'But I don't think it's quite what Gabriel meant by peace and quiet.'

'Of course she did,' said Fen comfortably. 'Percipient lady, my sister-in-law.'

'You've got your relationships all sorted out again, then?'

'Yes. I was a stupid, melodramatic idiot, suffering from arrested development, but I'm better now.'

'Good.' Joe smoothed her damp hair back from her forehead. 'Tell me, were Adam and Gabriel married before they moved into the Stables?'

'No.' Fen thought a bit. 'They were engaged, I know, because I was home for the party to celebrate it—the very day, now I come to think of it, that they started talking about a wedding. Why?'

Joe slid out of bed, pulled out a drawer in the tallboy, and brought out a box. 'I had planned to produce this last night, with candles and champagne, the whole nine yards. But fate conspired against me.'

'Is it a ring?' said Fen faintly.

'No, it's a gun! At least it could be, by the look on your face. Open it, darling, it won't bite.'

The ring was set with a square ruby, flanked either side with two small diamonds. Fen gazed at it, then held it out to Joe.

'You don't want it?' he demanded.

'Of course I want it,' she said impatiently. 'But you're supposed to put it on my finger.'

Joe's eyes locked with hers. 'I was waiting to see which finger you voted for. If you're taking it as a present I'll put it on your right hand, but if it goes on the left you have to mean it.'

'Mean what?'

'That you're committed to me and no other, Miss Dysart.'

'Oh, I see. Third finger, left hand, then.' She

smiled at him radiantly as it slid on as though made for her. 'It fits. Which is good. Because I'm not taking it off.'

'Unless we add another ring to that finger some time,' he said casually.

Fen gazed at him in silence for a moment. 'People don't get married so much these days,' she said at last.

'They do in your family.'

'True.'

'So because you are, as you said, Dysart twice over, I think your parents will like the living-together arrangement if you sport some kind of official badge,' said Joe, kissing her.

'The old Fen Dysart would probably have flared up over that,' she said, returning the favour. 'But I've grown up quite a lot lately. I love you, Joseph Tregenna, and will be honoured to wear this ring for ever, with or without another one to go with it.' Fen's eyes narrowed at the look on Joe's face. 'What now?'

'Before you commit yourself,' he said, sighing heavily. 'I've got a confession to make.'

She tensed. 'You're married!'

'No. I'm all yours, Fenny. But my name isn't Joseph. It's Josiah, after my grandfather.'

'*What?*' she said incredulously, and flung her arms round him, laughing. 'And you were angry with *me* for being secretive. Oh, well, a rose by any other name and all that.'

'Does that mean you love me just the same?' he demanded.

'I must do if I'm willing to marry a man with a name like that!' Fen gave him a deliberately possessive kiss. 'But the females of my family are all heirs to the Dysart legacy when it comes to love. Like my mother and my sisters I'm a one-man woman. And you're the man, Josiah Tregenna. My man,' she added with satisfaction.

'That I am,' said Joe, and began to show her, in a way they both liked best, how fervently he agreed with her.